A SECRET AFFAIR

BARBARA TAYLOR BRADFORD

A Secret Affair

HarperCollins*Publishers*

HarperCollins*Publishers*
77–85 Fulham Palace Road,
Hammersmith, London W6 8JB

Published by HarperCollins*Publishers* 1996
1 3 5 7 9 8 6 4 2

A catalogue record for this book
is available from the British Library

ISBN 0 00 225554 5

Set in Minion

Printed and bound in Great Britain by
Caledonian International Book Manufacturing Ltd, Glasgow

As always, for Bob,
with all my love

1

He was closing the small padlock on his duffle bag when a deafening explosion brought his head up swiftly. He listened acutely, with accustomed practice, fully expecting to hear another bomb exploding. But there was nothing. Only silence.

Bill Fitzgerald, chief foreign correspondent for CNS, the American cable news network, put on his flak jacket and rushed out of the room.

Tearing down the stairs and into the large atrium, he crossed it and left the Holiday Inn through a back door. The front entrance, which faced Sniper Alley, as it was called, had not been used since the beginning of the war. It was too dangerous.

Glancing up, Bill's eyes scanned the sky. It was a soft, cerulean blue, filled with recumbent white clouds but otherwise empty. There were no warplanes in sight.

An armored Land Rover came barreling down the street where he was standing and skidded to a stop next to him.

The driver was a British journalist, Geoffrey Jackson, an old friend, who worked for the *Daily Mail*. "The explosion came from over there," Geoffrey said. "That direction." He gestured ahead, and asked, "Want a lift?"

"Sure do, thanks, Geoff," Bill replied and hopped into the Land Rover.

As they raced along the street, Bill wondered what had caused the explosion, then said aloud to Geoffrey, "It was more than likely a bomb lobbed into Sarajevo by the Serbs in the hills, don't you think?"

"Absolutely," Geoffrey agreed. "They're well entrenched up there, and let's face it, they never stop attacking the city. The way they are sniping at civilians is getting to me. *I* don't want to die from a stray rifle shot covering this bloody war."

"Me neither."

"Where's your crew?" Geoffrey asked as he drove on, peering through the windscreen intently, looking for signs of trouble, praying to avoid it.

"They went out earlier, to reconnoiter, while I was packing my bags. We're supposed to leave Sarajevo today. For a week's relaxation and rest in Italy."

"Lucky sods!" Geoffrey laughed. "Can I carry your bags?"

Bill laughed with him. "Sure, come with us, why don't you?"

"If only, mate, if only."

A few minutes later Geoffrey was pulling up near an open marketplace. "This is where the damn thing fell," the British journalist said, his jolly face suddenly turning grim. "Bleeding Serbs, won't they ever stop killing Bosnian civilians? They're fucking gangsters, that's all they are."

"You know. I know. Every journalist in the Balkans knows. But does the Western alliance know?"

"Bunch of idiots, if you ask me," Geoffrey answered and parked the Land Rover. He and Bill jumped out.

"Thanks for the ride," Bill said. "See you later. I've got to find my crew."

"Yeah. See you, Bill." Geoffrey disappeared into the mêlée.

Bill followed him.

Chaos reigned.

Women and children were running amok; fires burned everywhere. He was assaulted by a cacophony of sounds . . . loud rumblings as several buildings disintegrated into piles of rubble; the screams of terrified women and children; the moans of the wounded and the dying; the keening of mothers hunched over their children, who lay dead in the marketplace.

Bill clambered over the half-demolished wall of a house and jumped down into another area of the marketplace. Glancing around, his heart tightened at the human carnage. It was horrific.

He had covered the war in the Balkans for a long time, on and off for almost three years now; it was brutal, a savage war, and still he did not understand why America turned the other cheek, behaved as if it were not happening. That was something quite incomprehensible to him.

A cold chill swept through him, and his step faltered for a moment as he walked past a young woman sobbing and cradling her lifeless child in her arms, the child's blood spilling onto the dark earth.

He closed his eyes for a split second, steadied himself before walking on. He was a foreign correspondent *and* a war correspondent, and it was his job to bring the news to the people. He could not permit emotion to get in the way of his reporting or his judgment; he could never become involved with the events he was covering. He had to be impartial. But sometimes, goddamnit, he couldn't help getting involved. It got to him occasionally . . . the pain, the human suffering. And it was always the innocent who were the most hurt.

As he moved around the perimeter of the marketplace, his eyes took in everything . . . the burning buildings, the destruction, the weary, defeated people, the wounded. He shuddered, then coughed. The air was foul, filled with thick black smoke, the smell of burning rubber, the stench of death. He drew to a halt, and his eyes swept the area yet again, looking for his crew. He was certain they had heard the explosion and were now here. They had to be somewhere in the crowd.

Finally, he spotted them.

His cameraman, Mike Williams, and Joe Alonzo, his soundman, were right in the thick of it, feverishly filming, along with other television crews and photographers who must have arrived on the scene immediately.

Running over to join the CNS crew, Bill shouted above the din, "What the hell happened here? Another bomb?"

"A mortar shell," Joe answered, swinging his eyes to meet Bill's. "There must be twenty or thirty dead."

"Probably more," Mike added without turning, zooming his lens toward two dazed-looking young children covered in blood and clinging to each other in terror. "The marketplace was real busy . . ." Mike stopped the camera, grimaced as he looked over at Bill. "A lot of women and children were here. They got caught. This is a real pisser."

"Oh, Jesus," Bill said.

Joe said, "The mortar shell made one helluva crater."

Bill looked over at it, and said softly, in a hard voice,

"The Serbs had to know the marketplace would be busy. This is an atrocity."

"Yes. Another one," Mike remarked dryly. "But we've come to expect that, haven't we?"

Bill nodded, and he and Mike exchanged knowing looks.

"Wholesale slaughter of civilians—" Bill began and stopped abruptly, biting his lip. Mike and Joe had heard it all before, so why bother to repeat himself? Still, he knew he would do so later, when he did his telecast to the States. He wouldn't be able to stop himself.

There was a sudden flurry of additional activity at the far side of the marketplace. Ambulances were driving into the area, followed by armored personnel carriers manned by UN troops, and several official UN cars, all trying to find places to park.

"Here they come, better late than never," Joe muttered in an acerbic tone. "There's not much they can do. Except cart off the wounded. Bury the dead."

Bill made no response. His brain was whirling, words and phrases racing through his head as he prepared his story in his mind. He wanted his telecast to be graphic, moving, vivid and hard-hitting.

"I guess we're not going to get our R & R after all," Mike said, a brow lifting. "We won't be leaving today, will we, Bill?"

Bill roused himself from his concentration. "No, we can't leave, Mike. We have to cover the aftermath of this, and there's bound to be one ... of some kind. If Clinton and the other Western leaders don't do something drastic, something especially meaningful, there's bound to be a public outcry."

"So be it," Mike said. "We stay."

"They'll do nothing," Joe grumbled. "They've all been derelict in their duty. They've let the Serbs get away with murder, and right from the beginning."

Bill nodded in agreement. Joe was only voicing what every journalist and television newsman in Bosnia knew only too well. Turning to Mike, he asked, "How much footage do we have so far?"

"A lot. Joe and I were practically the first in the marketplace, seconds after the mortar shell went off. We were in the jeep, just around the corner when it happened. I started filming at once. It's pretty bloody, gory stuff, Bill."

"*Gruesome*," Joe added emphatically.

Bill said, "It must be shown." Then, looking at Mike, he went on quickly, "I'd like you to find a place where we can film my spot, if possible one that's highly dramatic."

"You got it, Bill. When do you want to start rolling the tape?"

"In about ten minutes. I'm going to go over there first, talk to some of those UN people clustered near the ambulances, see what else I can find out."

"Okay, and I'll do a rekky, look for a good spot," Mike assured him.

William Patrick Fitzgerald was a renowned newsman, the undoubted star at Cable News Systems, noted for his measured, accurate, but hard-hitting reports from the world's battlefields and troublespots.

His fair coloring and clean-cut, boyish good looks belied his thirty-three years, and his tough demeanor stood him in great stead in front of the television camera.

He had earnest blue eyes and a warm smile that bespoke his sincerity, and integrity was implicit in his nature. These qualities underscored his genuine believability, were part of his huge success on television. Because he had this enormous credibility, people trusted him, had confidence in him. They paid attention to his words, listened to everything he had to say, and took him very seriously.

It was not for nothing that CNS treasured him and other networks coveted him. Offers for his services were always being made to his agent; Bill turned them all down. He was not interested in other networks. Loyalty was another one of his strong suits, and he had no desire to leave CNS, where he had worked for eight years.

Some time later he stood in front of the grim backdrop of burning houses in the marketplace, and his sincerity seemed more pronounced than ever. He spoke somber words in a well-modulated voice, as always following the old journalistic rule of thumb: *Who, when, where, what,* and *how,* which had been taught to him by his father, a respected newspaperman until his death five years ago.

"Thirty-seven civilians were killed and many others wounded today when a mortar shell exploded in a busy marketplace in Sarajevo," Bill began. "The mortar was fired by the Serbian army entrenched in the hills surrounding this battle-torn city. It was an obscene act of aggression against innocent, unarmed people, many of them women and children. UN forces, who quickly arrived on the scene immediately after the bombing, are calling it an atrocity, one that cannot be overlooked by President Clinton and the leaders of the Western alliance. UN officials are already saying that the Serbs must be forced to understand that these acts of extreme violence are unwarranted, unconscionable, and unacceptable. One UN official pointed out that the Serbs are endangering the peace talks."

After giving further details of the bombing, and doing a short commentary to run with the footage of the carnage, Bill brought his daily news report to a close.

Stepping away from the camera after his ten minutes were up, he waited until the equipment was turned off. Then he glanced from Mike to Joe and said quietly, "What I couldn't say was that that UN major I was talking to earlier says there *has* to be some sort of retaliation, intervention by the West. He says it's inevitable now. Public anger is growing."

Joe and Mike stared at Bill doubtfully.

It was Joe who spoke, sounding entirely unconvinced.

"I've heard that before," he said and shook his head sadly. "I guess this disgusting war has turned me into a cynic, Billy boy. Nothing's going to happen, you'll see . . . it'll be status quo . . ."

But as it turned out, Joe Alonzo was wrong. The leaders of the Western alliance in Washington, London, and Paris had no choice but to take serious steps to stop the Serbs in their systematic slaughter of Bosnian civilians, or risk being the focus of public outrage and anger in their own countries.

Just two days after the mortar shell exploded in the marketplace, the alliance sent in NATO warplanes to attack the Serbian army in the hills of Sarajevo.

It was August 30, 1995. The bombing began in earnest that day, and it was the biggest attack of the war. There were more than 3,500 sorties in the short space of two weeks, and even Tomahawk Cruise missiles were launched in the assault.

At the end of three weeks, the Serbians had begun to back down, withdrawing their heavy weaponry from the Sarajevo hills at the edge of the city, and making sounds about peace negotiations.

Because of the NATO attack and later developments, Bill Fitzgerald and the CNS crew remained in Bosnia, their week of rest and relaxation in Italy postponed indefinitely.

"But we don't really care, do we?" Bill said one evening when the three of them sat at a large table in the communal dining room of the Holiday Inn.

"No, of course we don't," Mike answered. "I mean, who cares about missing a week in Amalfi, relaxing with a couple of beautiful girls. Nobody would *mind* missing that, certainly not I. Or Joe." He shrugged. "After all, who gives a damn about sun, sea, and sex. And wonderful pasta."

Bill chuckled.

So did Joe, who said, "Me, for one. I give a damn." He grinned at the cameraman, who was his best buddy, then addressed Bill quietly. "I was certainly looking forward to our trip. And you were fixated about Venice, Bill, come on, admit it."

"Yes, it's true, I was. And I plan to make it to Venice soon. Maybe in the next month or two."

It was late September and relatively quiet out on the streets of Sarajevo; the fighting was less intense, with only sporadic sniping and fewer forays into the city on the part of the bloodthirsty Serbs. The entire foreign press corps were fully aware that the intense NATO retaliation had worked far better in curbing the Serbs than the words of appeasement the West had been uttering thus far.

Bill said, "I think things *are* going to ease up here, and very soon."

From their expressions, Mike and Joe were obviously disbelieving, and they did not respond.

Looking at his colleagues intently, Bill added, "With a little luck, this war should end soon."

Joe, ever the cynic, ever the pessimist, shot back, "Want to bet?"

"No, I don't," Bill replied swiftly. "You can never really tell what's going to happen with the Serbs. They talk out of both sides of their mouths."

"And shoot from the hip with both hands. Always fast on the draw, the fucking maniacs," Joe exclaimed.

"They started this war and they're only going to end it when it suits them. When they get what they want."

"Which is most of Bosnia, if not, indeed, all of it," Bill said. "This war's always been about territorial greed, as well as power, racial bigotry and ethnic cleansing."

"Greed, power, and hatred, a pretty potent combination," Mike murmured.

The cameraman glanced at his plate of food, his expression glum. He grimaced and put down his fork; his nose curled in distaste. "The soup was watery and tasteless, now this meat is greasy and tasteless. Jeez, this damn curfew has been getting to me more than ever lately. I hate having to eat here every night. I wish we could find somewhere else."

"There's nowhere else to eat in Sarajevo, nowhere that's any better, and you know we can't go out at night anyway," Bill reminded him. "Besides, it's difficult driving without any streetlights." Bill stopped, sat back in his chair, suddenly feeling worried about Mike and Joe. They rarely complained about anything; lately they had done nothing but complain to him. He couldn't say he blamed them. Living conditions in Bosnia never improved, only got worse. He thought of the line he had heard when he first came to the Balkans at the out-set of the conflict. It had been told to him by a reporter from a French news magazine and he had never forgotten it: *A day in Bosnia is like a week anywhere else; a week is like a month, a month is like a year.* And it was true. The country was wearing and wearying. It killed the soul, drained the spirit, and damaged the psyche. He was itching to get out himself, just as Mike and Joe were.

"It's not much of a menu, I'll grant you that," Joe suddenly said, and laughed hollowly. "It's always the same crummy food every night, that's the problem."

"Most people are starving in Bosnia," Bill began and decided not to continue along these lines.

All of a sudden Mike sat up straighter and announced, "Personally, I aim to be in the good old U.S. of A. in November, come hell or high water. I plan to be out on Long Island for Thanksgiving if it's the last thing I ever do. I want to be with my mom and dad, my kid brother and sister. It's been too long since I've seen them. I'm certainly not going to be in this godforsaken place, that's for sure."

"I know what you mean, old buddy," Joe said. "Me . . . I'd like to be in New Jersey for *my* turkey dinner. With my folks. I don't want to spend Thanksgiving in Bosnia either. Screw that!" Joe threw Bill a pointed look, and finished with, "Let's tell Jack Clayton we want out, Billy boy."

"Sure, I'll do it tomorrow. No problem. I'm positive

our grateful and adoring news editor will understand your feelings, and Mike's, and mine. He'll tell us to hop a plane to Paris, any plane we can get, and to hell with the expense, and then board the first Concorde out of Paris to New York. Pronto, pronto. Sure, he'll tell us to do that."

"Sarcasm has never been your forte, Bill," Mike remarked with an engaging grin, then went on: "But very seriously, talk to Jack tomorrow. Our rest period is long overdue. Originally, we were supposed to have it in July, then it got shifted to August, and finally it was canceled altogether. We haven't been out of Bosnia, except for a few long weekends in Hungary, for *three months*. I happen to think that we've all reached the end of our individual bits of rope."

"Could be we have. And you're right, Mike, so is Joe. Our R & R has been postponed for too long now. We're all edgy. Look, the peace talks are about to start in Dayton in October. That's only a few days away. Things ought to be relatively quiet here during that period, so I can't see that there would be any problems. Jack'll just have to send in another news team, should anything serious erupt when we're gone."

"There could easily be trouble," Mike remarked in a thoughtful tone. "Just because the peace talks are on doesn't mean that the guns will be silent. Not here. Anything goes."

"Only too true," Joe agreed. "Let's not hold our collective breath on that one."

"I know Jack's a tough news editor, but he is fair. He'll agree to this. Don't forget, *we* elected to stay when the NATO bombs started falling at the end of August. Jack was very appreciative that we did." Bill paused, thought quickly, and made a sudden decision. "Let's plan on getting out of here in a week. How does that sound, guys? Okay with you?"

Mike and Joe stared at him, dumbfounded. Then they grinned and exclaimed in unison, "*Okay!*"

2

The light in the piazza was silvery, the sky leaden, frosty. A faint mist rising from the lagoon and the many canals swathed everything in a veil of gray on this cold winter's afternoon.

Bill Fitzgerald walked slowly across St. Mark's Square, not caring about the weather in the least. There had been too many abortive attempts on his part to get to Venice, and he was glad he had finally made it.

It was a relief to be here after life in the battlefields of Bosnia; also a relief that the tides and the winds were cooperating and Venice was not flooded, as it frequently was at this time of year. Even if it had been, he wouldn't have cared about that either. The Venetians always managed very well when the city lay under water, so why shouldn't he?

He had been coming here whenever possible for the past few years. It was relatively easy to get to Venice from most cities in Europe, which was where he invariably was, on foreign assignment for his network. And even after only a couple of days here he always felt considerably refreshed, lighter in spirit and uplifted.

La Serenissima, the Venetians called it, this city of churches and palaces floating on water, blazing with color and liquid light, brimming with treasures of art and architecture. Bill thought it was one of the most intriguing and evocative places in the world, its aspects bound to delight even the most jaundiced eye.

On his first visit twelve years ago, he had spent a great deal of time in many of those churches and palaces, gazing at the breathtaking paintings by Titian, Tintoretto, Veronese, Tiepolo, and Canaletto. These masterpieces touched his soul with their incomparable beauty and, thereafter, the Venetian school of painting was one of his favorites.

He had always wished he could paint, but he was not in the least gifted in that respect. His only talent was with words.

"He's kissed the Blarney Stone, that one," his maternal grandmother, Bronagh Kelly, used to say when he was growing up. "True," his mother would agree. "That's his gift, a way with words. And he writes like an angel. We must remember that the pen is mightier than the sword."

Bill was an only child. He had spent a lot of time with adults when he was young, and his lovely Irish grandmother, in particular, was a favorite of his. He had been especially attached to her.

When he was little she had held him spellbound with her stories of leprechauns, lucky shamrocks, and pots of gold at the end of the rainbow. Bronagh had left Ireland with her parents and a younger brother when she was eight, and had grown up in Boston. It was here that she had met and married his grandfather, a lawyer named Kevin Kelly.

"I was born in 1905, and what a birth it was, Billy!" she would exclaim. "I came into this world at the stroke of midnight on the twelfth of June in the middle of the most violent thunderstorm," she'd tell him. "And me darlin' mama said it was a bad omen, that storm." She always embellished the details of her birth with every retelling, obviously enjoying his rapt expression and widening eyes. "And indeed it's been a stormy life I've lived ever since, Billy," she would add, with a huge laugh, which led him to believe she had relished her stormy life.

His wife, Sylvie, had loved Grandma Bronagh as much as he had, and the two had become very close over the years. His grandmother had been a true Celt, spiritual, mystical, and a little fey. Sylvie had shared these traits, been very much like her in many ways.

His only regret, whenever he came back to Venice,

was that he had not brought Sylvie here before she died. They had put it off and put it off, and suddenly, unexpectedly, it was too late. Sylvie was gone. Who could have known that she would die like that? In childbirth, of all things in this day and age. "Eclampsia" it was called; it began with seizures and ended in coma and death.

Losing Sylvie was the worst thing that ever happened to him. She had been too young to die, only twenty-six. His grief had overwhelmed him; he had been inconsolable for a long time. In the end, he had managed to come to grips with it, throwing himself into work in an effort to keep that grief in check and at bay.

As he went toward the Basilica, his thoughts were still centered on Sylvie. She had died in 1989; the baby, a little girl, had lived. She was called Helena, the name he and Sylvie had chosen. Now six years old, she was the spitting image of her mother, an adorable creature who entranced everyone she met.

Certainly she was a great joy to him. Whenever he felt depressed and disturbed by the rottenness of the world, he had only to conjure up her face and instantly he felt better. She made life worth living, his beautiful child.

A fleeting smile crossed Bill's face, touched his eyes

when he thought of her. Because his job as a foreign correspondent took him all over the world, she lived with his mother in New York. Fortunately, he saw her frequently and the time they spent together was genuinely meaningful. She was a good little girl, spirited, intelligent and not too spoiled, although his mother did dote on her only grandchild.

He had just spent two weeks in Manhattan with them, after covering the start of the Bosnia peace talks in Ohio. He would go back again in December, to celebrate Christmas at his mother's apartment in the East Sixties. When he wasn't in the middle of a battlefield or covering a major story in some far-flung corner of the globe, Bill made a point of being with "my best girls," as he called them. There was nowhere else he wanted to be, especially on important occasions and holidays.

But this week in Venice was his time for himself. He needed it badly, needed to put himself back together after his three-month stint in Bosnia-Herzegovina. Bill felt diminished by the conflict he had witnessed in the Balkans, and he was depleted, weary of war, of the destruction and the killing.

He wanted to forget. Not that he ever really would forget any of it. Who could? But he might at least be able to diffuse some of those horrifying images, still so vivid, that had left such a terrible scar on his mind.

His best friend, Francis Peterson, a war correspondent for *Time* magazine, believed that none of the newsmen would ever be able to expunge the violent images of Bosnia. "They're trapped in our minds like flies trapped in amber, there for all time," Frankie kept saying, and Bill agreed with him. All of them had seen too much savagery; its imprint *was* indelible.

Francis and Bill had met at Columbia University's School of Journalism in 1980, and they had been fast friends ever since. They were often covering the same wars, the same stories, but even when they were not, and were in different parts of the world, they stayed in constant touch.

Francis was currently assigned to Beirut, but he would be arriving in Venice in an hour or two, and they would spend a few days together. Later in the week, Frankie would fly to New York to celebrate his father's seventieth birthday.

Bill was glad his old friend was able to join him. They were exceptionally close, shared the same interests and understood each other well, were usually on the same wavelength.

Suddenly Bill realized he was the only person in St. Mark's Square, alone except for flocks of pigeons. The birds flew around him, soaring up above the Basilica. Usually the square was the center of animation in Venice, teeming with people, mostly tourists from all over the world. Now he was its solitary occupant, and as he glanced about it seemed odd to him, strangely surreal.

As he continued to walk, he became aware for the first time of the unique paving in the piazza. In the past when he had strolled here, there had been hundreds and hundreds of pairs of feet covering it, obviously the reason he had never noticed it before now.

His eyes followed the flow of the pattern: flat gray stones covering most of the square, balanced on either side by narrow white marble bands set in classical motifs. At once he was struck by the way the motifs directed the eye and the feet toward the basilica. No accident, he thought, walking on. When he came to the church, he did not go inside. Instead, he turned right and went down the Piazzetta San Marco, which led to the water's edge.

For a long time Bill stood looking out across the lagoon. Sky and sea merged to become a vast expanse of muted gray, which soon began to take on the look of dull chrome in the lowering afternoon light.

It was so peaceful here it was hard to believe that just across the Adriatic Sea a bloody war still raged. Nothing ever changes really, Bill thought as he turned away from the water at last. The world is the same as it's always been, full of monsters, full of evil. We've learned nothing over the centuries. We're no more civilized now than we were in the Dark Ages. Man's monstrosities boggled his mind.

Hunching deeper into his trench coat, Bill Fitzgerald retraced his steps across the empty square. He began to hurry now as dusk descended, making for the Gritti Palace, where he always stayed. He loved its old-fashioned charm, comfort, and elegance.

The rain started as a drizzle but quickly turned into a steady downpour. Bill, increasing his pace, was almost running as he approached the side street where the front entrance to the Hotel Gritti Palace was located.

He sprinted around the corner of the street at a breakneck pace and collided with another person also moving swiftly. It was a woman. As her large-brimmed cream felt hat and her umbrella went sailing into the air, he reached out and grabbed hold of her shoulders to prevent her from falling.

Steadying himself, and her, he exclaimed, "Excuse me! I'm so sorry," and found himself staring into a pair of startled silvery-gray eyes. In Italian, he added, "*Scusa! Scusa!*"

She responded in English. "It's all right, honestly," and disentangling herself from his tight grip she ran after her hat, which was blowing down the street.

He followed her, outran her, caught the hat, picked

up the umbrella wedged against the gutter, and brought them both back to her. "I apologize again," he said.

Nodding, she took the hat and the umbrella from him. "I'm fine, really." She glanced at the hat. "And this isn't any the worse for wear either." She shook it and grimaced. "Just a *bit* splattered with mud. Oh well, never mind. Who cares? It was never my favorite hat anyway."

"I'm a clumsy fool, barreling around the corner like that. It wasn't very smart of me. Are you sure you're all right?" he asked in concern, unexpectedly loathe to let her go.

She proffered him a faint smile, slapped the hat on top of her dark curls, and sidled away from him, saying, "Thanks again."

He stood rooted to the spot as if paralyzed, watching her walk off when he wanted desperately to detain her, to talk to her, even invite her for a drink. He opened his mouth. No words came out. Seemingly, he had lost his voice, not to mention his nerve.

Suddenly he galvanized himself. Almost running up the street after her, he shouted, "Can I buy you a new hat?"

Without pausing, she called over her shoulder, "It's not necessary, thanks for offering, though."

"It's the least I can do," he cried. "I've ruined that one."

She stopped for a moment and shook her head. "No, really, the hat doesn't matter. 'Bye."

"Please slow down. I'd like to talk to you."

"Sorry, I can't. I'm late." She glided on, swung around the corner.

Bill hurried after her.

It was then that he saw the man coming toward her, waving and smiling broadly.

The woman increased her pace, waving back and exclaiming in Italian, "Giovanni, *come sta*?"

A moment later she was holding her umbrella high over her head so that the man she had called Giovanni could properly embrace her.

Disappointment surged through him. Immediately, Bill turned away, rounded the corner, and went down the street toward the Gritti Palace. He could not help wondering who she was. Certainly she was the most stunning woman he'd seen in a long time. Those luminous silver eyes set in a pale, piquant face, the head of tumbling dark curls, the elegant way she carried herself. She was beautiful, really, in a gamine sort of way. It was just his luck that she was apparently already spoken for. He would have liked to get to know her better.

3

They met in the bar of the legendary Gritti Palace, which faced the Grand Canal.

"It's great to see you, Francis Xavier!" Bill exclaimed, "Just great that you could make it." He enveloped his best friend in a bear hug.

As they drew apart after their rough, masculine embrace, Frank said, "And likewise, William Patrick. It's been too long this time around. I've missed you."

"So have I—missed you."

Still grinning at each other, they both ordered single malt scotch from the hovering waiter and sat down at a small table near the window.

"A lot of wars have been getting in the way," Frank went on, "and we seem to have been covering different ones of late."

"More's the pity we haven't seen the same action."

They exchanged knowing looks for a long moment, remembering the tough situations they had encountered together and had shared. Genuinely close since journalism school, the two men, who were not only friends but colleagues, understood each other on a very fundamental level. And each worried about the other's well-being. They had a great deal in common, always had had—a love of truth and the need to find it, traits which made them superlative newsmen; diligence, honesty, and a zest for adventure. Yet, despite the latter, both were cautious, fully aware of the dangers involved in their work. Whether together or alone on assignments, they always endeavored to minimize the risks they took in order to get the story.

Their drinks arrived, and after they'd clinked glasses, Frank said, "There's no way I'll go back to Bosnia, Bill."

"I know. And I don't blame you. I've sort of had it myself. How is it in Beirut?"

"Fairly quiet. At the moment, anyway. Things are improving, getting more normal, relatively speaking, of course. I don't think it will ever be the Paris of the Middle East again, but the city's perking up. Good shops are opening, and the big hotels are functioning on a more efficient basis."

"Hezbollah's still lurking, though."

"You bet! We have to live with the threat of terrorism around the clock. But *you* know that." Frank lifted his broad shoulders in a light shrug, his dark eyes narrowing. "Terrorism is more prevalent than ever. Everywhere in the world. The bastards are all over the place."

Bill nodded, took a sip of his drink, and leaned back in the chair, enjoying being with Francis Peterson.

Frank said, with a wide smile, "Let's change the subject, get to something more worthwhile. How's my little Helena?"

"Not so little, she's grown a tad. Which reminds me . . ." As he spoke Bill pulled out his wallet, removed a photograph, and handed it to Frank. "Your goddaughter wanted you to have this. She sends you hugs and kisses."

Frank stared at the picture Bill had just handed him. He smiled. "She's the most adorable kid, Billy, you're so lucky. I see she's still got that Botticelli look about her . . . positively angelic."

"To look at, yes, but she's mischievous, a bit of a scamp, my mother says." Bill grinned. "But then who wants a perfect kid?"

"A perfect kid, if there is such a thing, would be insufferable. How's Dru?" he asked, putting the photograph in his own wallet.

"Pretty good, thanks. You know my mother, Frankie, full of piss and vinegar and energy, and as loving of heart as she ever was. She sends you her love, by the way."

"When you speak to her, give her mine. Better still, I'll call her myself when I get to Manhattan, to say hello.

Incidentally, I'm sorry I couldn't get home when you were there. I had a really tough deadline for my piece on Lebanon. There was just no way I could take off at that time."

"I understood."

Frank went on, "I gather you weren't particularly impressed with the peace talks in Dayton."

Bill shook his head. "I wasn't. The Serbs are a diabolical bunch. Gangsters. They're never going to agree to a proper and *fair* peace treaty with the Bosnians, you'll see. As for all this UN talk about prosecuting some of the Serbs as war criminals, you can forget it. I assure you it will never happen. They're never going to get those butchers to the Hague to stand trial, for one thing. Just take my word for it. The Serbs are going to get away with their crimes."

"Tragic though it is, you're probably right, Bill."

"It's just wishful thinking on the part of the UN."

"I agree."

A small silence fell between them.

The two men sipped their drinks quietly, lost for a moment in their own thoughts.

They were a good-looking pair, both of them clean-cut and collegiate in their appearance. Any casual observer would have known immediately that they were Americans.

Frank was as dark as Bill was fair. He prided himself on being third-generation Irish-American, and Black Irish at that. He had a shock of dark hair, black eyes, and a fresh complexion. Like Bill, he was thirty-three, and currently single. His marriage to a television foreign correspondent, Pat Rackwell, one of the rising stars of her network, had foundered on the rocks of her career four years ago.

Fortunately they had had no children, and the divorce had been amicable enough. Whenever they ran into each other on a story, they pooled their information, their resources, and tried to be helpful whenever they could. Very frequently they had dinner together when they were in the same foreign city.

Breaking the silence, Bill said, "I heard a nasty comment about us the other day."

"Back in New York?"

"Yes."

"What was it?"

"That we're war junkies, you and I. That we love danger, love being in the thick of it, and that that's what gives us our jollies. We're characterized as being extremely reckless. A bad example."

Frank threw back his head and roared. "Who cares what people think! I bet it was one of your competitors at another network who made *those* lousy comments."

"As a matter of fact, it wasn't. It was one of the guys at CNS."

"Aha! He wants your job, William!"

"Yeah, he probably does." Bill hesitated for a second, then gave Frank a piercing look. "Do you think the odds *are* against us? That we will get killed one day, when we're covering a war in some godforsaken place?"

Frank was reflective. After a second he murmured, "So many journalists have lost their lives . . ." He let his voice trail off; his expression remained thoughtful.

"But we won't lose ours. I just feel it in my bones!" Bill asserted, his voice positive all of a sudden.

"You're absolutely right, it's just not in the cards. Anyway, you're bulletproof."

Bill chuckled.

"Furthermore, you're my lucky charm."

Bill cut in swiftly, saying, "Except that I'm not always with you these days, Frankie."

"True enough, just wish you were. We've had some experiences in the past, shared some highs and lows, haven't we? Remember the Panama Invasion?"

"How could I forget it? December of 1989. Sylvie had only been dead a few months, and I was so grief-stricken I didn't care what happened to me, didn't give a damn whether I lived or died."

"But you did care about me," Frank said in a low

voice, staring at his friend with sudden intensity. "I wouldn't be sitting here tonight if it hadn't been for you, Bill, you saved my life."

"You'd have done the same for me."

"Of course I would! But don't ever forget that I've always been very grateful."

"And so has the female population of . . . whatever city you're living in at the moment."

Frank grinned at his friend, said facetiously, "Aw shucks, Billy, don't start that again. I'm not the only newsman who likes a bit of female company occasionally. And what about you? You're not so shy with the girls either."

"There haven't been many women around lately, I'm afraid, not where I've been."

Frank nodded. "Sarajevo's hardly the place for a romantic interlude."

Bill confided, "Heard another thing in New York, Francis Xavier."

"Oh, yeah, and what's that? It obviously has something to do with me, from the tone of your voice."

"Sure does. Rumor has it you're suffering from a terminal Don Juan complex."

Frankie chuckled and went on chuckling. He was highly amused.

Bill smiled, feeling comfortable, relaxed, and more

at ease with himself than he had been for a long time. He knew that with Frank in Venice, for a few days he would be able to shake his depression, dispel the horrific images of war, and recharge his batteries completely.

Now Bill motioned to the waiter, ordered two more drinks, and said, "It's not such a bad reputation to have, when you think about it. After all no man can be a Don Juan unless women are interested in him."

"Only too true. As they say, it takes two to tango. By the way, I ran into Elsa in Beirut a few weeks ago."

"Elsa?" Bill frowned, looking puzzled.

"Don't tell me you've forgotten Elsa Mastrelli, our guardian angel from Baghdad."

"*That* Elsa! Oh, my God, how is she?"

"The same. Still covering wars for her Italian news magazine, still playing Florence Nightingale, ministering angel, and earth mother all rolled into one. At least, so I've been told."

"She was really great. Is she still as attractive?"

"Yes. Well, slight correction necessary here. Elsa has matured, looks more interesting, more experienced, even a bit war-weary, tired. But yes, she's still a knockout, a good-looking woman with a lot of savoir faire. In other words, she's grown up. We had a quick drink at the Commodore and reminisced about Baghdad."

"That was one hell of a time in our lives, Frankie!" Bill exclaimed animatedly. "My God, I'll never forget it . . . January of 1991. Only four years ago, but it seems so much longer, don't you think?"

"It sure does. We took some real chances, Billy, in those days."

"We were only twenty-nine. And very daring."

"Also very stupid, if you ask me." Frank threw Bill a pointed look. "No story's worth dying for."

"No, it isn't. But we didn't even think about dying, let's face it. And our Baghdad coverage made both our careers. Weren't we lucky that CNS was the only television network allowed to stay on in Baghdad? And that you and Elsa were the only print journalists given permission to stay on with us to cover the Gulf War?"

"All thanks to you and that enterprising producer of yours, Blain Lovett. What happened to him, is he still with CNS?"

"No, he went to NBC, then moved over to CBS. He's still there, doing very well, but no longer going out on foreign assignments. By choice, I guess."

"He was great, the way he networked. What a wheeler-dealer he was."

Bill grinned, remembering his former producer. "He had his act down pat, making his important contacts before the war started. Long before. And the Iraqis loved his schmoozing. He charmed a lot of them well before the conflict began and so they favored him. And we were home free when holy hell finally did break loose."

"I'll never forget the day he told you that our Iraqi minders were letting CNS bring in all that television equipment from Jordan," Frank said. "Including that satellite phone. I, for one, was flabbergasted."

"So was I, Frankie, and where would we have been without it? That phone was our only link to the outside world, and CNS was the only network getting coverage out for the world to hear and see."

"It did wonders for CNS, pushed them to the top of the pile in live news coverage in particular. And actually, Billy, we were fortunate to come out of that debacle alive, all things considered, and all those direct hits the hotel took. And there was Elsa, what a terrific little trooper she was . . . "

Frank paused as he realized that he had lost Bill's attention. "What's wrong?" he asked.

"Nothing."

"Something's wrong. You're not listening to me. And you have the strangest expression on your face."

Bill turned to Frank. "I don't want you to look now, but it's that woman over there. At the other side of the bar. Did you see her come in?"

"How could I fail to miss her? She's the only other person here except us. So, what about her?"

"I almost knocked her over earlier today. Collided with her this afternoon as I barreled around the corner, on my way back to the hotel. I chased her hat."

"*Chased her hat?*"

"Oh never mind, and don't look at me like that."

"Like what?"

"As if I'm nutty."

"Well, you are a bit crazy, Billy, and so am I, thank God. Life's too damned hard not to be slightly crazy from time to time. How else are we going to deal with all the stress and tension? Anyway, what about this woman?"

"I was very taken with her this afternoon. I wanted to get to know her better."

"I can't say I blame you. She's interesting-looking. Is she Italian?"

"I don't think so, even though she looks as if she might be. I'm pretty sure she's an American, certainly she sounds it. Anyway, her hat flew off as we collided, so I ran after it. I also ran after her as she thanked me and walked off. I wanted to invite her to have a drink with me. It's funny, Frankie, but I didn't want her to go."

"Why didn't you ask her to have a drink?"

"I tried to, but she was hurrying, almost running. I

---

was right behind her, and so naturally I saw her with the man she was meeting. Just my luck that she's involved with someone. For all I know he might even have been her husband. I watched them embrace. Still, I must admit I've thought about her for the past few hours, off and on."

"There's only one thing to do."

"What's that?"

"Go over and invite her to have a drink with us," Frank suggested. "You'll get the lay of the land pretty quickly."

"I guess you're right." As he spoke, Bill pushed himself to his feet and strode across the bar, walking in a direct line toward the young woman.

She looked up from a notebook she was holding and smiled when she saw him. "Hi!" she said, sounding friendly.

"Since you wouldn't let me buy you a new hat, could I at least buy you a drink?" Bill began. "My friend and I would love you to join us for . . . drinks *and* dinner."

"That's really nice of you both, but I can't. I'm waiting for a friend. I have a previous engagement," she explained.

Bill looked crestfallen. "Just my luck, er, er, our luck. Well . . ." His voice trailed off and he half turned to go, and then he swung around to face her again. "You're an American, aren't you?"

"Yes, I am. From New York."

"So am I."

"I know."

"My name's Bill—"

"Fitzgerald," she supplied, eyeing him, looking suddenly amused. "I know who you are; in fact, I watch your newscasts all the time, Mr. Fitzgerald."

"Call me Bill."

"All right."

"And you are?"

"Vanessa Stewart." She thrust out her hand.

Leaning forward, Bill took hold of it, and shook it. He discovered he did not want to let it go. "I have a great idea," he said and finally released her hand.

"You do?" She raised a dark brow and her large silver-gray eyes were quizzical as they focused on him intently.

Bracing his hands against the back of the chair and leaning forward, drawing closer to her, Bill said, "We must be the only three Americans in Venice at the moment, so we *must* spend tomorrow together."

"*Tomorrow?*" Her brows drew together. "Why tomorrow?"

"It's Thanksgiving."

"Oh, my God, I'd forgotten."

"Well, it is. Thursday, November the twenty-third. And it would be a crime if the only three Yanks in Venice didn't celebrate this most American of all holidays together. Join me and my friend, Francis Peterson of *Time.* Come on, what do you say?"

"Very well, I'll join you, but only on one condition."

"What's the condition? Shoot."

"That we have a proper Thanksgiving dinner with turkey and all the traditional trimmings."

Bill's face lit up in the most engaging way, and he grinned boyishly. "You've got a deal!" he declared.

She smiled up at him. "Then I'll be happy to come, thank you very much. Shall we meet here in the bar?"

"Good idea. Champagne first, and then on to our turkey dinner with all the trimmings. What time?"

"Seven. Is that all right?"

"Perfect." From the corner of his eye Bill saw the Italian, Giovanni, entering the bar. He inclined his head and politely took his leave. Moving away from her table swiftly, he retraced his steps across the room.

Frank had been watching Bill alertly, and now he said, "What happened?"

"She can't join us tonight. For obvious reasons. The Italian is on the scene again."

"Is that him over there now? The guy she met this afternoon?"

"Yes. Giovanni. However, she has agreed to have dinner with us tomorrow night."

Frank looked impressed. "That *is* an accomplishment, old buddy. How did you do it?"

"I reminded her that it's Thanksgiving, pointed out that we were more than likely the only three Americans in Venice, and added that it would be a crime if we didn't celebrate the holiday together."

"And she agreed?"

"On one condition."

"And what's that?"

"A turkey dinner. She wants a traditional Thanksgiving meal with all the usual trimmings."

"You didn't promise it, did you?"

"Sure I did. Why are you looking skeptical, Francis?"

"Where the hell do you think you're going to find a turkey? In Venice, of all places, for God's sake! This is pasta land, Billy."

"I know, and don't worry. Just trust me."

"But Bill, a *turkey*—"

"Did I ever let you down in Baghdad? Who's the one who always managed to find the most delectable stuff in that war-torn city . . . from Johnnie Walker to cans of corned beef."

"Well, you were pretty good," Frank admitted, grinning.

"I know what I'm doing," Bill remarked. "I booked us a table at Harry's Bar tonight. And we'll go there again tomorrow. Everyone from Arrigo Cipriani, the owner, and the maître d' to the youngest busboy knows me well. Please believe me, Harry's Bar will make us a real American Thanksgiving dinner. They'll get a turkey, no matter what. After all, the mainland's not far away."

"I know better than to argue with *you*, Billy. And what's the lady's name?"

"Vanessa Stewart. She's from New York. She knew who I was."

Frank threw him an amused look. "Good God, don't sound so surprised, Bill. The whole of America knows who you are. Your face is in their living rooms every day of the week."

4

"Do you think she's stood us up?" Frank said the following evening. He and Bill were sitting in the bar of the Gritti Palace, waiting for Vanessa Stewart to arrive. He glanced at his watch. "It's twenty past seven."

"Stood *us* up! *Never*," Bill answered in a jocular tone, with a quick laugh. "Two dashing war correspondents like us. Good Lord, Frankie, don't you know by now that we're irresistible?"

When Frank merely threw him a sharp look and made an exasperated noise, Bill added in a more sober tone, "But seriously, I don't think she's the type to do that."

"What makes you so sure?"

"I just am, trust me on this," Bill replied firmly. "I thought she seemed like a serious person yesterday, and although we spoke only briefly, I detected something in her, an air of breeding. I know she would have phoned us here by now if she weren't coming, to make some sort of polite excuse. I sensed that she was not flaky, not the flighty kind at all."

"If you say so. And I guess it's a woman's prerogative to be late," Frank responded. Then he and Bill exchanged swift looks and promptly sprang to their feet as Vanessa Stewart appeared in the doorway of the bar. She hurried in, gliding forward at a rapid pace.

The young woman, who was of medium height and slender, wore a burgundy-colored outfit made of crushed velvet and carried a matching wool coat. The narrow velvet pants were paired with a loose, tunic top, which, with its square neckline and long sleeves cut wide at the cuffs, had a medieval look about it. Strands of amethyst-and-ruby-colored glass beads were twisted into a choker around her neck, and small gold medallions gleamed at her ears.

Both men wore admiring expressions as she drew to a standstill in front of them, a look of concern on her face.

"Sorry I'm so late," she said in an apologetic voice, shaking her head. "So rude of me, but it was unavoidable. I was delayed at a meeting this afternoon. When I got back to the hotel it was late and I had to change. I didn't want to lose any more time by calling you in the bar. I thought it best just to dress and hurry down."

"Are you staying here?" Frank said.

"Yes, I am."

"It's not a problem," Bill exclaimed, wanting to put

her at ease. Smiling warmly, he went on, "Vanessa, I'd like to introduce you to my friend Francis Peterson of *Time* magazine. And Frankie, this is Vanessa Stewart."

"It's very nice to meet you," Vanessa said, shaking Frank's outstretched hand.

"And I you," the journalist answered, offering her a welcoming smile, thinking how personable she was and how attractive, in an offbeat way. Bill had described her to him as being gamine, and it was true, she did have a roguish, saucy kind of charm. With her huge gray eyes in that small, piquant face and her short, curly, dark hair she looked very young and vulnerable. She reminded him of someone, someone he couldn't quite place.

Vanessa put her coat on a chair and sat down.

Bill said, "Would you like a glass of champagne or do you prefer something else?"

"Oh, champagne's lovely, thank you." She settled back in the chair and crossed her long legs.

Champagne was poured, and after they had all clinked glasses Bill said, with unconcealed curiosity, "You mentioned you were delayed in a meeting. So are you here on business?"

"Yes, I am." Vanessa cleared her throat, and went on, "I'm a designer. Of glass. I get most of it blown here. On Murano, to be exact. So I'm coming and going all the time."

"Are you a New Yorker?" Frank asked.

"Yes. I was born there."

"Do you live in Manhattan?"

She nodded. "In the East Fifties."

"Good old New York," Frank murmured. "There's nowhere else like it in the whole world."

Bill said, "What kind of glass do you design?"

"Vases, fancy bottles, big plaques and plates, decorative objects mostly, things to put on display. But I also make jewelry, like these beads." She touched the choker on her neck and explained, "But mostly I create objects for the home. Last year Neiman Marcus launched a line of mine, which I designed exclusively for them, and it's been a big success. That's why I'm here right now, to supervise the new collection."

"Oh, so it's currently being made, is it?" Bill said.

"Yes, at one of the oldest glass foundries on Murano. There's nothing like Venetian glass, in my opinion anyway. I think it's the best in the world."

"Where did you study in the States?" Frank probed.

"The Rhode Island School of Design, but also here in Venice. I did a graduate course for a year."

"So you lived in Venice!" Bill exclaimed. "How I envy you. I love this city."

"So do I." Vanessa's face took on a glow; she smiled at him. "La Serenissima . . . the Serene Republic, and it's so aptly named, isn't it? I always feel truly content here, peaceful, yet very alive. Venice is a state of being, I think."

Bill looked at her closely. He knew exactly what she meant about Venice. Struck by her openness, he nodded, returned her smile, and found himself staring into her luminous gray eyes. He averted his face, picked up his drink, and took a quick swallow. He felt suddenly self-conscious of his awareness of her, of his sexual attraction to her.

Frank, conscious of Bill's sudden discomfort, said, "And tell me, Vanessa, where do you normally spend Thanksgiving?"

"With my mother, if we happen to be in the same place. And sometimes with my father, if Mom's away. It depends on the circumstances."

"You make it sound as if your mother travels a lot," Frank remarked, raising a brow questioningly.

"She does."

"For pleasure or business?" he asked, still probing.

"Her work."

"And what does your mother do?"

"She's an actress."

"In the theater?"

Bill sipped his champagne, leaning back in the chair, listening, thinking that Frankie was asking too many questions. But at the same time he wanted to hear her answers. She intrigued him in a way no woman had for the longest time.

"Oh, yes, my mother works in the theater, and in films," Vanessa said.

"Would we know her?" Bill leaned forward, focused his attention on her.

Vanessa laughed. "I think so. My mother is Valentina Maddox."

"Is she really!" Bill cried. "Well, now that I know who she is I must admit you have the look of her, a very strong resemblance, in fact."

Frank said, "And Audrey Hepburn many years ago, when she was in *Sabrina*. That's who you reminded *me* of when you first walked in. Hasn't anybody ever told you that you look like her?"

Vanessa was still laughing. She nodded.

Frank now asked, "Aren't your parents divorced?"

"Yes. But they're still friends, and they see each other from time to time. They both live in New York. Well, Dad does. My mother's really a gypsy, flitting around the world, going wherever her work takes her."

"Do you have any brothers or sisters?" Bill inquired.

"No." Vanessa sat up straighter and looked from Bill to Frank, then began to laugh again. "What a lot of questions you both ask!"

"We're journalists. It's our job to ask questions," Frank replied.

They walked to the Calle Vallaresso, just off San Marco, where Harry's Bar was located.

It was a cold night. Frost hung in the air and ringed the moon, a clear silver sphere in an ink-dark sky. Cloudless and clear, it was littered with a thousand tiny pinpoints of brilliant light.

The streets were relatively deserted. Only a few people were about. As the three of them walked along, they could hear the clatter of their own shoes on the cobblestones.

"Hollywood couldn't have done it better," Bill remarked at one moment, glancing at the sky. "Hung that moon up there like that. What a fantastic film set Venice is, actually."

Vanessa exclaimed, "That's what my mother used to say when she came to visit me! She has always thought Venice to be the most theatrical of places in the whole world."

"She's right," Bill said, taking hold of Vanessa's arm, guiding her as they went down the narrower streets in the direction of the famous restaurant. He loved the closeness of her, the scent of her perfume. It was light, floral. Enticing. Just as she herself was enticing. He was

---

very drawn to her, just as he had been yesterday, but tonight the feeling was more powerful.

They walked on in silence for a few seconds until Bill said, "I suppose you know all about Harry's Bar."

"Not really," she responded. "I went there with my parents, but only once. Didn't Ernest Hemingway make it his hangout?"

"He did, yes, along with a lot of other writers and journalists and celebrities. It was founded in the nineteen thirties, when an American, Harry Pickering, the now famous Harry, borrowed money from a hotel barman. The bartender was Giuseppe Cipriani, and when Harry paid him back he gave him additional money to open a bar. And *voila*! The restaurant was born."

"I love stories like that," Vanessa said, and then shivered slightly, drew further into her coat.

"Are you cold?" Bill asked solicitously.

"No, no, I'm fine."

Frank, who had been silent during the walk to the restaurant, announced, "There's Harry's Bar, straight ahead. We'll be inside in a minute."

They were given a royal welcome when they walked into Harry's Bar. Once they had shed their coats, they were escorted to one of the best tables at the back of the room. "Welcome, Signore Fitzgerald," Arrigo Cipriani said. "And 'appy Thanksgiving."

"Thanks, Arrigo. Now, how about some Bellinis to celebrate the holiday?"

"Good idea," Frank said.

"That'd be lovely," Vanessa agreed, and once they were alone she turned to Bill, and said, "I've forgotten what a Bellini is. I mean, I know it's champagne but what's in it besides that?"

"Fresh peach juice."

"Now I remember! They're fabulous."

A great deal of camaraderie had developed between them in the short time they had known each other. Vanessa had taken their probing questions at face value, had not been offended, and they in turn had been struck by her attitude, realizing what a good sport she was. And so the gaiety and banter continued at Harry's, only to be interrupted when a waiter arrived at their table, presenting the menus with a flourish.

"I ordered a special main course for us all last night," Bill explained.

"Si, Signore Fitzgerald, I know. But you didn't order a first course."

"True, I didn't. What do you suggest?"

"What about *risi e bisi*, I know you like it." Looking at Vanessa and then at Frank, the waiter continued, "It's a wonderful risotto. Mmm." He kissed his fingertips. "Rice with peas, ham, and Parmesan cheese. Delicious."

"Sounds good enough to eat," Frank joked.

Bill grinned at Vanessa. "It is good. I think I'll have it. How about you?"

"All right. Thank you."

"We'll all have it," Frank added. "And let's take a look at the wine list, please, Antonio."

"Si, Signore Peterson." The waiter nodded and departed.

Vanessa pushed back her chair and said, "Excuse me for a moment," and left the table, heading for the ladies' room.

Bill leaned over and said to Frank, "So, what do you think of her?"

"She's lovely, and you were right, she's not a bit flaky. In fact, I think she's a very nice young woman, one who's rather serious by nature."

Bill said, "I like her."

"It's more than *like*, Bill, that's too soft a word."

"What do you mean?"

"You're bowled over by her, and you're going to get involved with her. She with you."

"I'm not so sure."

"About yourself? Or her?"

"Both of us."

Frank smiled broadly, and a knowing glint entered his black Irish eyes. "Oh Bill, my boy, take my word for it, you are heading for the big one here. She's irresistible to you, has all the things you love in a woman. As for her, she can't take her eyes off you. She's intrigued, flattered by your interest in her, and she hangs onto every word you say."

"I think you exaggerate."

"Trust me, I don't. I've got eyes in my head, and I've been watching you both for almost two hours now. You're both trying to hide it, but you're falling for each other."

"I wonder who that Italian is? Giovanni?" Bill muttered.

"We can't very well ask her. Anyway, she's not wearing any rings, at least not a wedding ring, only that crested signet on her little finger."

"But that doesn't mean anything these days. And she does spend a lot of time here, she said so."

"That doesn't mean anything either, Billy. I'm telling you, that young woman —" Frank stopped as Vanessa glided up to the table.

The two men rose, and Bill helped Vanessa into her chair.

Once she was seated, she smiled across at him, and said, "You reminded the waiter you'd ordered a main course last night. Not a turkey?"

"Of course it's a turkey. I ordered a traditional Thanksgiving dinner for us, and fortunately they were able to oblige. After all, that was your condition, Vanessa."

She stared at him for a long moment, and shook her head slowly. Her eyes twinkled mischievously when she finally murmured, "But I was only teasing. I never thought for one moment that you'd find a turkey in Venice . . . "

Bill stared at her.

Vanessa's touch was featherlight as she rested her hand on his arm. "You see, I *wanted* to spend Thanksgiving with you . . . with or without a turkey."

5

What Francis Peterson had predicted finally came to be.

Bill and Vanessa fell in love.

As Bill said much later, they probably did so on Thanksgiving night at Harry's Bar, although it took them several days to acknowledge their feelings.

During the Thanksgiving weekend they got to know each other better. In fact, they were a threesome, since they spent Friday and Saturday with Frank.

For these two days Vanessa became their guide, showing them places in Venice that not even Bill, the Venice aficionado, knew about. These were small, unique art galleries, museums and churches off the beaten track, bars and cafés known only to the Venetians themselves, shops where the best bargains were to be had.

At Bill's insistence, she took them out to Murano, where she did much of her work. They went to the island by *vaporetto*, a water taxi that took only seven minutes to get there.

Bill and Frank both wanted to see her designs, and so they visited the ancient glass foundry where her glass pieces were handblown. Both men were impressed by her stunning designs, her talent and creativity, and they realized she was a true artist.

That evening, at her request, they escorted her to a cocktail party given by an old friend of hers from her student days, who owned a palazzo on the Grand Canal situated diagonally across from the Gritti Palace. They needed a gondola to get there.

The two newsmen found the slightly ramshackle palace an amazing place, and were fascinated by its many treasures. Carlo Metzanno, their host, was an interior designer, and he had given the massive, centuries-old palace a great deal of style and elegance. As he showed them around, he explained the provenance of many of the art objects, paintings, and antiques. Prominently displayed were several extraordinary pieces by Vanessa. These were fluid, sinuous, and impressive.

The three of them stayed at the cocktail party for an hour, mixing with a colorful group of people including a couple of local artists, a famous French movie star, a playwright from London, and an American architect.

When they left the palazzo, the same gondola that they had hired for the evening took them to the Giudecca, the narrow sliver of an island across the Canale della Giudecca. Vanessa had invited them to dinner, and she had booked a table at Harry's Dolci, the charming and intimate "little sister" of Harry's Bar. After their meal they strolled over to the Hotel Cipriani for espressos and stregas before going back to Venice in the gondola. "We've become the three musketeers," Frank said as they took their seats, settling back to enjoy the ride to the Gritti Palace. "We're now old pals." Bill and Vanessa laughed, and Bill said, "I think that's swell."

Bill had planned what he termed "an adventure" for Saturday night. Once again, a gondola was hired for the evening, and this carried them down the narrow winding backwaters of Venice until they arrived at an old house that looked like a hole in the wall. It turned out to be a marvelous family restaurant, one Bill knew well, which was a popular eating place favored by Venetians in the know.

It was a gay evening filled with bonhommie. They laughed and joked, exchanging a lot of amusing banter. A considerable amount of genuine affection flowed between them. The two men had grown quite close to Vanessa, and she to them.

"Here's a toast, then," Frank said as the dinner drew to a close. "To dear friends—old and *new*." He clinked his glass of red wine to Bill's glass and then Vanessa's. Smiling at her genially, he added, "You're a good sport, kid, the way you've put up with us. Especially *me*, with all my questions. I've enjoyed being with you for the last couple of days. You've been like . . . a breath of fresh air."

Vanessa colored slightly, the flush rising from her neck to touch her face. Frank had teased her a lot, and now she was touched by his compliments, his unexpected courtliness.

"What a nice thing to say, Frank, thanks, and I've enjoyed *your* company."

"I'm going to miss you both," Frank went on, looking from Vanessa to Bill. "Most especially you, William Patrick. Battlefields are not the same without you."

"I know," Bill replied, his eyes focused on his best friend. "I'll miss you, too, but who knows, we may well be covering the same story in the next few months."

"Could be," Frank said. "I hope so."

As they left the restaurant a short while later, Vanessa shivered and moved nearer to Bill, who put his arm around her protectively and drew her close against him.

Venice in winter, and especially in the evening, was mysterious, even frightening. The gondola glided down many dark waterways, heading for the Gritti Palace. Mist rose up from the murky canals, and there was no noise except for the slap of the oars as they hit the water. Everything was shadowy, eerie in the dim light.

On either side of the narrow waterways, buildings

loomed up like strange inchoate monsters under the threatening sky. At times the mist was more like fog, thick and almost impenetrable. The dampness clung to them, seemed to penetrate their clothes.

The three friends stayed huddled in the gondola, shivering, fighting the cold, talking quietly until they reached the hotel.

"I'm glad we're back," Vanessa said with another shiver as Bill helped her to alight at the small dock in front of the Gritti Palace. "There are times when Venice at night frightens me, fills me with foreboding—" She cut herself off, feeling suddenly foolish. After all, she had two men to protect her, not to mention the muscular gondolier who looked like a prizefighter.

Since they each had their rooms on different floors, they said good night in the lobby.

Frank, who was leaving the following morning for Milan and then a direct flight to New York, kissed Vanessa on both cheeks. He gave Bill one of their customary bear hugs.

"See you, William," he said nonchalantly, walking to the elevator. Suddenly, he paused, turned around, and looked at them both for a split second, the expression on his face unexpectedly serious.

"Take care of each other," he said and disappeared behind the sliding doors of the elevator.

*   *   *

Bill and Vanessa remained standing in the lobby, staring at each other.

Vanessa's eyes were full of questions as she murmured, "What an odd thing for him to say—" She stopped, her gaze still riveted on Bill.

"Not really," Bill answered quickly. Then, after the merest hesitation, he went on, "You see, he knows how I feel about you."

"How is that?"

"I'm very . . . *drawn* to you, Vanessa."

She was staring up at him; she nodded. "I guess he knows I feel the same way."

"You do?"

"Oh, yes, Bill."

Bill inclined his head slightly. "So, Frankie *was* right. He sensed it from the beginning. He was quite positive he knew exactly how we *both* were feeling."

"He's very astute." She spoke in the softest of voices.

"He is. Do you want a nightcap? Or something hot, maybe? Hot lemon tea?"

"Not here, though," Vanessa said.

"Your room or mine?"

"Oh yours, please," Vanessa answered with a small, shy smile. "You have a suite, mine is nothing so grand."

Putting an arm around her shoulder, Bill led her to the other elevator at the far end of the lobby. The minute the door closed, he did what he had been wanting to do for the past three days. He took her in his arms and kissed her.

Vanessa kissed him back, and with such intensity he was momentarily startled. When the elevator came to a halt, they quickly pulled apart. As they stepped out, he noticed her flushed face. She was usually so pale.

Drawing a finger down one side of her cheek, he leaned into her and whispered, "You're burning up. Hot to the touch."

She looked at him swiftly but said nothing.

With their arms wrapped around each other, they walked along the corridor to his suite. After letting them in, Bill closed the door with his foot. Shooting the bolt with one hand, he pulled her into his arms with the other. Once more they clung together, kissing with growing fervor.

Suddenly Bill held her away from him and said, "Let's take off our coats." So saying, he helped her out of hers, struggled to shrug off his trench coat, and threw both on a nearby chair.

Silently Bill took hold of her hand tightly, led her into the adjoining bedroom and over to the bed. Vanessa seated herself on the edge of it, all the time watching him as he bent down and took off her shoes, first one and then the other.

After kissing each foot, he slid his hand under her wide, flared skirt, stroking her leg, moving up until his fingers caressed her inner thigh.

"Bill?"

"Yes?"

"Let's get undressed."

A half smile touched his mouth. With swiftness he rose, took her hands in his and pulled her to her feet, so that they were facing each other. Vanessa moved closer, placed her arms around his neck, kissed him on the mouth passionately. As she did so, he reached behind her and unzipped her wool skirt.

The skirt fell to the floor, lay in a swirl of purple at her feet. She stepped away from it, then swung back to him, her eyes focused on him with intensity.

Bill looked at her closely. What he saw surprised and pleased him. Her face was flushed, full of desire, and her silvery eyes brimmed with longing. For him.

Roughly Bill pulled her to him, bent his face to hers, and kissed her deeply. He slid his tongue into her mouth, let it graze hers, and she did the same, exciting him more than ever with her fervor and unabashed desire. He felt the blood rush to his face; he was aroused as he had not been aroused for years. He wanted her so much, had wanted her for days, and now he felt as though he would explode. He had an enormous erection. He pressed himself against her; she bent to his will, letting her whole body flow against his.

Leaning away from her slightly, he looked down at her breast, touched it gently. How taut it was under the thin silk blouse. Fumbling, he undid the first few buttons, put his hand inside her blouse. He kissed her breast, then sucked on the hardening nipple.

"Please, let's lie down, Bill."

Clinging to each other they staggered to the bed. She began to take off her blouse, but he stopped her.

"Let me do it," he said in a low voice. "I want to undress you. Please, darling."

She nodded. Her eyes never left his face as he opened her blouse. After slipping it over her shoulders, he began to kiss her neck, her arms, and brought his mouth back to her breast. As his tongue tantalized the nipple, he undid her bra. At last both of her small, rounded breasts were free and he buried his head between them.

Bill could feel Vanessa's strong hands in his hair, smoothing and stroking, massaging his neck and shoulders. He heard her soft moans as he moved from one breast to the other, tenderly kissing and touching them, inflaming himself as well as her.

After a moment he sat up, looked down at her stretched out on the bed. How exciting she was to him, so vulnerable in her delicate beauty. She wore a lacy, black garter belt and sheer, black stockings. Carefully he undid the suspenders and rolled down each stocking, took off one, then the other. His eyes ravished her body, so trim and lean, yet shapely. Unfastening the garter belt, he slipped it off.

She stared up at him, her eyes wide and unblinking. "I want you," she said in a husky voice.

He nodded, stood up, threw off his clothes haphazardly, lay down next to her. Taking her in his arms, he kissed her eyes, her lips, her ears. "I want to kiss every part of you," he whispered against her hair.

"I'd like that," she murmured.

He slid down the bed, brought his mouth to the core of her. She responded wildly, crying his name. Her body suddenly convulsed in a spasm, and she grasped his shoulders hard, gasping as she did so.

Before he could stop himself, Bill was astride her, lying on top of her. Both his hands reached up into her dark curls, and he covered her mouth with his, touching his tongue to hers. He needed to take her to him. Now. Without further delay. Bracing his hands on either side of her he raised himself up, stared down into her eyes.

"Yes," she cried. "Oh, yes, Bill."

His hands left her hair, moved on to fondle those taut breasts with their erect nipples. He pushed his hands under her back, then her buttocks, lifting her closer to him, fitting her body to his. He was harder than ever and slid inside her easily.

And she welcomed him with her warm and pliant body, cleaving to him, thrusting up to him. She became welded to him. She moved her legs, threw them around his back, as high as they would go, so that he could shaft deeper and deeper into the warm, soft core of her. And they found their own rhythm, moving faster and faster until they were frenzied.

Bill thought his heart was going to burst. He sank deeper and deeper into her until he was entirely enveloped by her. "Vanessa," he gasped. "Vanessa."

"Yes, Bill!" she cried. "Don't stop."

He brought his mouth to hers again, and holding her tightly in his arms, they came to a climax together, sharing their ecstasy. And their joy in each other was unparalleled.

6

"That was all too quick," Bill said, encircling her with his arms, pulling her closer to him. "I'm afraid I was overanxious."

"No, you were wonderful."

"I've wanted us to be together like this since the other afternoon, when I almost knocked you over."

"So have I."

"Really and truly, Vanessa?"

"Yes, honestly."

He felt her smile against his chest. Before he could stop himself, Bill asked, "Who's Giovanni?"

She swiveled her eyes to look up at him. "How do you know his name?"

"I heard you greet him the other afternoon, just after I'd chased your hat."

"I see. He's an old friend . . . we met when I was doing my graduate course here. We became close, he helped me in lots of ways."

"Are you lovers?"

"No." Vanessa hesitated, then added, "Giovanni lives with someone, has for several years . . . another man."

"Oh." Bill cleared his throat, and after a moment he said, "We asked you lots of questions, Frankie and I, but we didn't ask your age, being the gentlemen that we are. But how old are you, actually?"

"Twenty-seven. Soon to be twenty-eight. And you're about thirty-five, aren't you?"

He laughed. "Thanks a lot! And no, I'm thirty-three," he replied and kissed the top of her head. "You said you were staying another four days. That means you're leaving on Wednesday. Correct?"

"Yes, I have to work at the glass foundry on Monday and Tuesday."

"Can I see you in the evenings? Can we be together until you leave?"

"Of course, I want that too, Bill."

"Listen, I'm coming to New York in December. For the Christmas holidays, in fact. Are you going to be around?"

"Yes." There was a small pause before she continued, "Bill, there's something I must tell you."

He heard an edge in her voice all of a sudden and he frowned. "Go ahead."

Vanessa took a deep breath and plunged. "I'm married."

For a moment Bill did not respond, and then he moved up on the pillows.

Vanessa struggled free of his embrace, turned to face him.

They stared at each other intently.

Vanessa saw surprise mingled with hurt on his face.

"Don't be angry with me. Don't look at me like that," she cried.

"How do you expect me to look, for God's sake? I'm disappointed, Vanessa. You lied to me."

"No I didn't, we never mentioned my marital status."

"You lied by omission."

"What about your private life, Bill? Is there a woman in *your* life? You don't need a piece of paper to make a commitment to someone. Making it legal doesn't necessarily make the bonds any stronger, the attachment greater. Do you live with a woman?"

"No."

She sighed.

He said, "Do you live with him?"

"Sort of . . ."

"What does that mean?"

"He's away a lot. And I go to my studio in the Hamptons a great deal of the time. I have a barn and a cottage in Southampton. So we're not together often."

"And when you are? Is it a proper marriage?"

She shrugged.

"Do you sleep with him?" he pressed.

Vanessa did not respond.

"Your silence is golden . . . it means that you do."

"It's not a good marriage—"

His hard laugh stopped her short. "Ah, the misunderstood married woman!" he exclaimed.

"No, it's not like that!" She leapt off the bed, ran into the bathroom, and came back a moment later wrapped in a terry cloth robe. Seating herself on the edge of the bed, she took hold of his hand.

Bill looked at her, his face taut. He was trying to come to grips with his emotions. After making such passionate love he had been euphoric, a feeling he had long forgotten existed. And he had felt at ease with this young woman who had come so unexpectedly into his life. He knew he wanted to get to know her better, to spend time with her. Her announcement that she was not free had been a bombshell.

Vanessa exclaimed, "Please, Bill, don't be angry. Let me explain."

"I'm not angry, and go ahead, be my guest. *Explain*," he said and there was a sarcastic note in his voice.

Ignoring this, Vanessa said, "Peter's a lawyer, a show-business lawyer and very successful. He's away a lot, mostly in Hollywood. It wasn't like that at first, but his business has grown. And I'm traveling, too. I suppose, in a way, we've grown apart a bit. But he's a good man, and he's been very supportive of me, as I have of him. So we sort of . . . muddle through. It's not a great marriage, but it's not a bad one either."

"Have you never thought of leaving him?"

She shook her head. "He's a good man, as I just said. I wouldn't want to hurt him."

"What about you, Vanessa? Aren't you entitled to have a happy relationship with a man?"

"I don't think it's possible to build one's happiness on someone else's unhappiness."

"I know what you mean."

"In any case, Peter would fall apart if I left him. I just couldn't have his pain on my conscience."

"Do you have children?"

"No, sadly we don't."

"How long have you been married?"

"Four years."

"Do you still love him?"

"I care about him—" She came to a halt, looked thoughtful, finally confided, "Peter's been in my life for such a long time. We're good friends, and we have a lot in common. He's always encouraged me in my work, my career, never stood in my way. He's a nice person. I like him. I respect him, and I love him. But—"

"You're not in love with him, is that what you're trying to say?"

"Yes." Vanessa bit her lip and shook her head. "I mean, how could I be here with you like this if I were?"

Bill laid his head back against the pillows and closed his eyes. A small sigh escaped, and without opening his eyes, he said softly, "I just wish you'd told me you were married, that's all."

"I wanted to," Vanessa said. "I intended to, and then we started to have such a good time together. I liked you so much. I wanted to be with you, and I just thought you'd lose interest if you knew I had a husband."

He said slowly, "You should have been straightforward with me."

"Have *you* been with me?"

He sat up swiftly and stared at her. "Yes, I have. There isn't a woman in my life. You know I'm widowed. My God, the whole world knows I'm widowed. And I haven't had a really good relationship since Sylvie died. Oh, yes, there've been a few women, but I've never fallen in love, or had a meaningful relationship since my wife died six years ago. To tell you the truth, I thought that you and I might have something going for us, that this was the beginning of something special. I want a good relationship, Vanessa, I want to have another chance at happiness." He shrugged. "I guess I was wrong to think it might be with you."

Vanessa said nothing, looked down at her hands twisting nervously in her lap.

The awkward silence grew.

At last she said, "How do you *really* feel about me, Bill? Be scrupulously honest."

He gave her a hard penetrating stare. "We've just made passionate love, and you ask me that?" He gave a short laugh, pursed his lips. "Obviously I'm overwhelmingly attracted to you, turned on by you. I enjoyed making love with you. Let's face it, we've just had wonderful sex. I like being with you. I admire your talent. As I told you in the lobby a short while ago, I'm very taken with you, Vanessa."

"And I am with you, Bill. So much so I haven't really been able to think straight for the last couple of days. All I know is that I just want to be with you. Whenever we can. You're a foreign correspondent, you're obviously going to go back to Bosnia or somewhere else, and I have my own career . . ." She shook her head, and tears brimmed in her eyes. "I thought we would see each other whenever we could, be together as often as possible and . . . see what happens."

"Let things work themselves out in their own time, is that what you mean?"

"Yes. Whenever my mother was facing difficulties, she would always say to me, 'Vanny, life takes care of itself and a lot of other things as well. And usually it's for the best.' That's still her philosophy, I think."

Bill looked at her thoughtfully. "So, what you're saying is that you want to have an affair with me? A secret affair. Because you don't want your husband to be hurt. Am I correct?"

"It sounds terrible when you put it that way."

"But it *is* the truth. And as a newsman, I *am* a seeker of truth."

Vanessa shook her head, biting her lip again. Slowly, tears trickled down her cheeks.

"Oh, for God's sake, don't start crying!" he said, and reached for her, pulled her into his arms. He flicked her tears away with his fingertips, then tilted her face to his. Softly, he kissed her on the mouth.

When he stopped, she said, "Please tell me you're not angry with me, Bill."

"I'm not angry. Only selfish. I always want things my way, like most men. And listen, you haven't committed a crime. Anyway, why should you stick your neck out for me?" He laughed. "I'm always in harm's way . . . a bad risk."

"Don't say that!" she cried, her eyes flaring.

Tightening his grip on her, he brought his face closer to hers and whispered, "I *want* to be your lover. Now why don't you take off that robe so that I can start practicing."

7

It was an extraordinary day, clear, light-filled. A shimmering day. The sky dazzled. It was a perfect blue, unmarred by cloud, and the sun was brilliant above the rippling waters of the lagoon. The air was cool, but not as cold as it had been over the past few days, and the mist had dissipated.

On this bright Sunday afternoon, Bill and Vanessa walked through the streets and squares for several hours, holding hands, hardly speaking but comfortable in their mutual silence. Both were swept up in the beauty of Venice. They walked on past the Accademia, down the Calle Gambara into the Calle Contarini Corfù, until they came at last to the Fondamenta Priuli-Nani.

"Of course I remember this area now," Vanessa said, turning to Bill, smiling up at him as they headed down the street. "That's the old boatyard of San Trovaso, where gondolas are repaired," she continued, gesturing to the decrepit-looking buildings ahead of them. "I came here once with my father. He wanted to see the Church of San Trovaso. It's very old, if I remember correctly."

"Yes, it is," Bill replied. "It was built in the tenth century, and that's where I'm taking you now, actually. To the church. I want to show you one of my very favorite paintings. It's by Tintoretto. And incidentally, gondolas are also *made* at the San Trovaso boatyard, it's one of the last of the building yards left in Venice."

"They've all more or less disappeared. So many of the old crafts have become defunct," she murmured, sounding regretful. "But, thank goodness, glassblowing hasn't!" she finished with a light laugh, grinning at him.

They continued on past the boatyard, and walked up over the Ponte delle Meravegie, the bridge of marvels. Within seconds they were approaching the Church of San Trovaso, its cream-colored stone walls and slender bell tower rising up above the trees, a sentinel silhouetted against the cerulean sky.

After they had entered the church, Vanessa and Bill stood quietly for a moment, adjusting their eyes to the dim light and the overwhelming silence. They both genuflected, and Bill threw Vanessa a swift glance but made no comment, realizing that she also must be a Catholic. They slowly moved forward, walking down the nave toward the altar.

Immediately, Bill brought Vanessa's attention to the two paintings hanging on either side of the choir. "Both are by Tintoretto," he explained. "The last two pictures he ever painted. In 1594. Come on, let me show you the one I love the most." A moment later they were in front of *The Adoration of the Magi,* Tintoretto's great masterpiece.

"I've always liked this particular Tintoretto myself," Vanessa volunteered. "It's absolute perfection. The colors, the images, the incredible brushwork."

"Wasn't he marvelous," Bill said, "A towering genius." He fell silent, simply stood staring at the picture, rooted to the spot, unable to tear his eyes away.

At this moment it struck Vanessa that Bill was mesmerized by the painting. Several times she threw him a surreptitious look, but she made no comment, not wanting to break the spell for him; she understood how moved he was by this great work of art.

Finally dragging his eyes away from the painting, he said, "When I look at this Tintoretto, and the other treasures in Venice, and consider man's incredible talent, his ability to create incomparable beauty, I can't help wondering how man can also be the perpetrator of an evil so stupendous it boggles the mind. It's hard to reconcile the two."

"But the two have always coexisted," Vanessa answered, putting her hand on his arm. "Venice *is* the total personification of visual beauty. It's there for us to *see,* to take pleasure from, wherever we look. The art, the architecture, the many different treasures that have been accumulated here over the centuries, the very design and layout of Venice itself—" She paused for a split second before she added softly, "You have just come out of Bosnia, where you witnessed inhumanity and savagery, cruelty beyond belief. And those images must still be in your mind, Bill. How can you not make comparisons?"

"You're right, yes, I know that," he said, and turning away from the painting at last, he took hold of her arm and led her down the nave, back to the front door of the ancient church. "I suppose the beauty of paintings and music help to make the hard realities of life . . . bearable."

"I think so."

Once they were outside in the sunlight, Bill blinked and shook off the images of the Balkans war that had momentarily overtaken him. He exclaimed, "It's such a long time since I've taken a gondola up the Grand Canal. Shall we do it, Vanessa? It's still the most spectacular trip, isn't it?"

"Absolutely. And I'd love it. It's ages since I've done it myself, and I guess the Grand Canal personifies Venice, doesn't it? Besides, I find gondolas a very relaxing way to travel."

Bill felt a sudden rush of happiness surging up in

him. He knew it was because of Vanessa, her presence by his side. He put his arm around her, hugged her to him. "I'm glad we met, I'm glad we're here today in Venice. I'm glad we made love last night. I'm glad we have a few more days together." He stopped, tilted her face to his and looked at her, a faint smile briefly touching his mouth. "Whatever your circumstances are, Vanessa, you're the best thing that's happened to me in a long time." He kissed the tip of her nose. "Clandestine though it must be, I want our affair to continue." His eyes searched hers questioningly.

She nodded. "So do I. Whenever we can, wherever we can," she answered, and reached up, threw her arms around his neck, pulled his face to hers, and put her mouth on his. "There," she added, "sealed with a kiss."

He laughed, and so did she, and with their arms wrapped around each other they walked back the way they had come. Retracing their steps past the old boatyard, they went down the narrow streets until they came again to the Campo dell' Accademia, where Bill hired a gondola to take them back to the Gritti.

Immediately they were seated, Bill put his arm around Vanessa again and pulled her closer to him, realizing as he did that in only a few days this woman had come to mean so much to him. It didn't seem possible that he could care so deeply for someone other than Helena or his mother, but he did now. And it was all very sudden at that.

For her part, Vanessa was thinking similar things, and wondering how her life would ever be the same again. It wouldn't, she was positive. Not ever again. Because of Bill.

The two of them sat with their backs to the gondolier, who was in the prow. They were facing St. Mark's Basin, the vast expanse of water that rolled up to the quay.

Directly in front of them were the island of San Giorgio, the Church of the Salute, and the Dogana, the beautiful domed customs building. These buildings, known as the three pearls to the entrance of Venice, were turning golden in the late afternoon sunlight.

"The light of Turner," Bill said, leaning forward intently, looking at the sky. "Vanessa, do you see the changing light? It's gone a peculiar yellow, the yellow Turner captured so perfectly on canvas. I've always loved the paintings he did of Venice."

"So have I. And this view is the very best," she replied. "The entire city floating on water, the water changing with the light. The whole scene is . . . dream-like . . ." Vanessa paused, thinking how truly lovely it was. Magical, almost otherworldly. It moved her; she felt the unexpected prick of tears in her throat, touched as she was by the beauty of this city.

Sky and shifting water merged, golden, then irides-
cent in the lowering light of the afternoon. All the colors of Venice were reflected now in the Grand Canal as
they floated along it, heading for the hotel.

Fading sunlight caught the cupolas of the basilica,
streaking them to silver, touching the pale colors of the
palazzos, giving the pink, terra-cotta, ocher, and pow-
dery yellow a dusky, golden cast. All these colors of La
Serenissima blended in a delicate mix, with just the hint
of green here and there. And everywhere the sense of
blue . . . blues bleeding into watery grays.

The gondola slid slowly up the Grand Canal, past
the ancient palazzos jammed close together, almost
higgedly-piggedly, tall and narrow. The houses were
built on stilts, just as Venice itself was built on pilings
pounded into the sand, silt, and rock centuries ago.

Sinking, she thought, they say it's sinking. And it
was, very slowly, even though some of the rot had been
stopped.

Vanessa stared at the palazzos, all of them full of
priceless treasures, works of art by the great masters,
paintings, sculptures, silver and gold objects, tapestries,
furniture. How terrible if it all sinks, she thought with a
shudder. What a tragedy that would be.

Bill increased the pressure of his arms around her,
and she leaned back against him. She was falling in love

with him. She shouldn't, but she was, and she didn't know how to stop herself.

They sat in the bar of the Gritti Palace and had hot chocolate, tiny tea sandwiches, and small, delicious cakes. It was growing dark outside, the bright sunlight of earlier had dulled to leaden gray, and a wind had blown up, but it was warm inside, comfortable in the bar. They were enjoying being together, getting to know each other better.

At one moment Vanessa murmured, "You haven't really said where you're going from here, Bill. Is it Bosnia again?"

He was silent for a moment and then he nodded, his face suddenly grim. "But only to do a wrap-up. I won't be there longer than three or four days, thank God."

"The war must have been awfully hard to cover . . . I saw such horrors whenever I turned on the television. I can't imagine what it was like to actually be there."

"It was hell."

"It affected you . . . I know from the way you spoke with Frank."

"Yes, the war did affect me, change me. I've been a witness to genocide . . . the first war and genocide since the last war and genocide in Europe. That was in the thirties when the Nazis started persecuting the Jews, exterminating them, along with the gypsies and anyone else they thought needed killing off. I never imagined it could happen again, or if it did, that the world would permit it." He shook his head and shrugged. "But the world *has* permitted it, and the civilized world, at that. Excuse me, Vanessa, I shouldn't use that term. Nobody's civilized as far as I'm concerned. All any of us have is a thin veneer; scratch that in the right place and a monster will appear." He gave her a hard look, and went on, "As a newsman I have to be dispassionate, objective and balanced. Like a bystander, *watching*, in a sense."

Vanessa nodded. "Yes, I understand, but that must be very hard for you."

"It is now. At one time I could move around at will, from battlefield to battlefield, without being upset or disturbed. Bosnia has altered all that. The savagery, the butchering of innocent, unarmed civilians. My God, it was horrific at times . . . what we all witnessed. There are no words strong enough or *bad* enough to describe it."

Vanessa was silent.

After a moment she reached out and took hold of his hand, held it tightly in hers, knowing better than to say a word.

Bill was quiet for some time. He finally said, "I'm going to be doing a special on terrorism. I have two months to put it together. We'll start filming in January through February, so that we can air it in March."

"That's why you're not going to be based in Sarajevo?"

"Correct. I'll be traveling through the Middle East."

"Will . . ." She tightened her grip on his hand and leaned into him. "Will we be able to meet?"

"I hope so, darling. I'm counting on it."

"Shall we make Venice our place of rendezvous?"

He squeezed her hand. "I think that's a brilliant idea."

"When are you coming to New York in December?"

"About the fifteenth. I have two weeks' vacation due." He searched her face. "That won't present a problem will it, meeting in New York?"

"No, of course not. And I've a favor to ask," she said, smiling.

"Then ask it."

"Can I meet your daughter?"

"Do you want to *really*?"

"Yes, Bill, I do."

"Then you've got a date. I'll take you all to lunch. Helena, my mother, and you. It'll be great, having my three best girls out on the town with me."

8

Vanessa Stewart had always prided herself on her honesty. It was not only an honesty with those people who occupied her life, but with herself. For as long as she could remember, she had despised prevaricators and even those who merely half-fudged the truth.

But now on this icy December day she had to admit to herself that she had not been honest for a long time. At least, not as far as her private life was concerned.

There was no longer any question in her mind that she had lied to herself about the state of her marriage. And lied to Peter, too, by not forcing him to admit that their marriage was floundering, not working on so many different levels.

I've lied by omission, she thought, remembering the line Bill had used in Venice some ten days ago now. By not being open with Peter, I've only compounded our basic problem. I'm as much at fault as he is. And there was a problem. More than one, in fact.

Face the truth, Vanessa suddenly admonished herself. Be a big girl, accept things the way they are now. They're not the same as they once were; they haven't been for a long time.

A distracted look settled on her face as she focused on her marriage, the drawings spread out in front of her now forgotten. She and Peter no longer communicated very well, hardly at all, really. The shared confidences of their courtship and the early days of their marriage had long since been abandoned. Their sex life was practically nonexistent. And whenever they did make love these days it was usually because they had quarreled. Peter had always believed that this was the best way of making up. Certainly the easiest for him, she now thought.

But quite aside from this, they spent a great deal of their time apart. They were always in different places, or so it seemed to her.

And their interests were very different. They had grown apart . . . as they had grown in different ways.

It's no marriage at all, Vanessa thought. It's just a sham, truly it is. We stay together out of . . . *what*? Suddenly she did not know why they stayed together. Unless it was out of habit. Or loyalty. Or lack of a better place to go. Or someone else to go to. Or laziness. Which one of these reasons it was, she had no idea. Perhaps it was all of them in combination.

Placing the pencil on top of her drawing board, Vanessa leaned back in the tall chair where she sat and stared out of the huge window in front of her. Her mind was racing.

Her design studio was in a building downtown in Soho, on the corner of Mercer and Grand. It was a fifth-floor loft looking south, and she had fallen in love with it at first sight because of its spaciousness and extraordinary natural light.

The view from her window was familiar to her, but it never failed to please her. She had not grown tired of looking out at her own special corner of Manhattan. The splendid nineteenth century buildings were lined up before her eyes, while behind them the pristine twin towers of the World Trade Center, all black glass and steel, pierced the afternoon sky.

Two centuries juxtaposed, she thought, as she did every so often. The past. The present. The future.

The future. Those words danced in her head.

What was *her* future?

Was it to continue to live this lie with Peter? This lie that was their marriage ... no, the remnants of their marriage.

Or was she going to leave him?

Is that what the future held? A life without Peter Smart, the only man she had ever known, except for Bill

Fitzgerald? Well, that wasn't quite the truth either, if she were scrupulously honest. There had been one other man in her life. Steven Ellis. Her college beau. Her first lover, her only lover until she had met Peter. And then married him.

And now Bill Fitzgerald was her lover. Her clandestine lover. Was it because of Bill that she was suddenly looking truth in the face? Had her relationship with him forced her to be honest for the first time in several years? More than likely. Yes, it's because of Bill and the way you feel about him, a small voice in her head whispered.

A deep sigh escaped her. She did not know what to do. Should she make Peter see their marriage for what it was, a sham? If she did, what would happen? And what did *she* want to happen? Peter might say they should start all over again, try to make a go of it. And where would she be then? Was that what she wanted? A future with Peter Smart?

What she had said about him to Bill was true. Peter was a good man, a decent human being. And he did love her in his own way. Furthermore, he looked after her well, and he had been extremely supportive about her work, had encouraged her career. Peter was a caring man in a variety of ways, and reliable, dependable, loyal.

And she was absolutely convinced he would be hurt and unhappy if she left him. He depended on *her* in so many ways.

Why would she leave Peter anyway?

Because of Bill?

Yes.

But Bill hasn't asked you to leave Peter. He hasn't made any kind of commitment to you, that insidious voice whispered. In fact, he rapidly agreed to an affair, a secret affair. He accepted the idea of being your clandestine lover. Actually, he suggested it, the voice added.

But Bill or no Bill, her life with Peter had grown . . . empty? *Yes.* Stale? *Yes.* Lonely? In many ways, *yes.* They didn't share anything anymore, at least that was the way she saw it, the way she felt. There was so much lacking in their relationship. For her, anyway. Maybe Peter felt differently. Maybe he expected less of marriage than she did.

And what did she want in a marriage?

Emotion. Love. Warmth. Companionship. True feelings shared. Sexual love. Understanding. Was that too much to ask of a man? Surely not. Certainly it was not too much for her to give.

Peter had not offered her many of these things lately, quite the contrary. And wasn't that one of the reasons she had ended up in bed with Bill in Venice?

Yes, the little voice answered. But it had also happened because she was overwhelmingly attracted to Bill. Falling in love with him? Yes, it was happening. Hadn't she known that days ago in Venice?

Falling in love, Vanessa thought. More like falling into madness.

It was dusk when Vanessa left her studio and got into the waiting radio cab that she had ordered earlier. As the driver headed uptown, her thoughts again turned to the problems in her life. Wrestling with them was not proving to be very fruitful; certainly she wasn't coming up with any answers for herself. The only thing she knew for sure was that her Venetian interlude with Bill, the feelings they had shared, had only served to point up the unsatisfactory relationship she had with Peter.

Comparisons, she thought, I hate comparisons. They're odious. But, of course, how could she not compare the emotional closeness she and Bill had enjoyed with the aridness of her life with Peter?

It suddenly struck her that Peter was denying her his love, himself, just as he had denied her a child. Instantly, she crushed that thought, not wanting to confront it, or deal with it now.

On the spur of the moment, she leaned forward and

said to the driver, "I need to make a stop on the way uptown. I'd like to go to Lord & Taylor, please."

"Okay, miss," the driver said, and turned left off Madison when they reached East Thirty-ninth Street. He headed west to Fifth Avenue, where the famous old store was located.

The driver parked the cab on the side street, but Vanessa walked around to Fifth Avenue and stood looking at the Christmas windows. They were always the best, she knew that from her childhood. The windows were full of wondrous mechanical toys, breathtaking scenes from famous fairy tales and the classics, magical to every child.

Pressing her nose against the window, as she had done when she was a child, she smiled inwardly, watching an exquisitely made toy ballerina, dressed in a pink tutu, pirouetting to the strains of "The Sugar Plum Fairy." The music was being piped out into the street, and it brought back such a rush of forgotten memories that Vanessa's throat tightened unexpectedly.

Her mother and father had always taken her to see *The Nutcracker* if they were in New York over Christmas, just as they had brought her here to see the store's windows before going inside to meet Santa Claus and confide her Christmas wish.

Sometimes they had not been in Manhattan at

Christmas, but in California or Paris or London, depending on her mother's current movie or play. Or what her father, Terence Stewart, was directing at the time. She was an only child, and they had always taken her with them on location or wherever they went. She had never suffered because of their theatrical careers; she had had a lovely, and very loving, childhood and had remained extremely close to her parents.

Eventually Vanessa turned away from the window, suddenly overcome by feelings of immense sadness and loneliness. An aching emptiness filled her, as it so often did. It was a feeling that threatened at times to overcome her. Somehow, she always managed to throw it off. She knew what it was—the longing for a child. But Peter did not want the responsibility of a child, and so she had buried the longing deep inside herself, sublimated the desire for a baby in her work. But, occasionally that terrible yearning gripped her, as it was doing now. She tried to still it, wishing it away.

Pushing through the swinging doors, Vanessa went into the store, her mind focusing on Helena, Bill's little girl. She was looking for something truly special. Helena was six, and there were so many things to buy for a child that age. Taking the escalator, she rode up to the children's department, spent ten minutes looking around and left empty-handed. Nothing had caught her eye.

As she hurried across the main floor, Vanessa stopped to buy tights and winter boot socks, then picked up eye makeup she needed before returning to the cab.

When she arrived at their apartment on East Fifty-seventh Street, Vanessa was surprised to find her husband at home. He usually never got in from his law office before seven in the evening at the earliest.

She shrugged out of her topcoat in the foyer and was hanging it up in the closet when he came out of their bedroom.

He was holding a couple of silk ties in his hand, and his face lit up at the sight of her. Smiling hugely, Peter said, "Hi, sweetie."

"You're home early," she answered, walking forward.

He nodded, kissed her on the cheek as she drew to a standstill. "I wanted to get my packing done before dinner."

"Packing?" A frown marred the smoothness of her wide brow. "Where are you going?"

"To London. Tomorrow morning. I have to see Alex Lawson. As you know, he's filming there at the moment. Anyway, his contract for his next two movies is finally ready, and I've got to go over it with him, walk him through it. It's a bit more complicated than usual."

"Oh, I see."

"Don't look so glum, Vanessa. I'll be back in ten days, certainly in time for Christmas."

"Does it take ten days to walk an actor through a contract? Or is he particularly dumb?"

"Vanessa! How can you talk like that about Hollywood's biggest heartthrob," he said and laughed a deep-throated laugh, amused by her comment. "You, of all people! Coming from a show business family as you do."

When she made no response and moved away, Peter took hold of her arm and gently turned her to face him. "I thought we'd go somewhere special for Christmas. Mexico . . . Bali . . . Thailand. Anywhere you want."

"But my mother will be in New York for Christmas . . ." Her voice trailed off. Suddenly she felt depressed.

"All right, then we'll stay here; it was just an idea. But no problem, no problem at all, sweetie." He went back into the bedroom.

Vanessa followed him, placed her Lord & Taylor shopping bag on the bed, and sat down next to it.

Peter spent a moment or two sorting ties, then he turned around and gave her a puzzled look when he saw the expression on her face. "What's the matter?" he asked, walking over to the bed, looming up in front of her.

She met his steady gaze with one equally as steady, but the expression on her face was thoughtful. Her husband was thirty-eight years old. Slim, attractive, a man in his prime. He had a genial personality, natural charm, and was popular both with his friends and clients. A brilliant lawyer, he had become highly successful in the past few years, and the success sat well on him. Peter Smart had everything going for him. And yet his personal life was abysmal. She ought to know; she shared it with him. It was empty, arid, pointless. As was hers. Didn't he notice this? Or didn't he care? Then it suddenly hit her like a ton of bricks: Was there another woman in his life? Is that why he had nothing to give *her* anymore?

"You're looking odd," Peter remarked in a quiet voice.

She cleared her throat. "I'm sorry you're going away; I'd hoped we could spend a quiet weekend together. I want to talk to you, Peter."

He frowned. "What about?"

"*Us.*"

"You sound serious."

"I feel serious. Look, you and I . . . things are just not right between us these days."

He gaped at her. "I don't know what you mean, Vanessa."

"What's our life about?" She gave him a penetrating stare. "We seem to be . . . drifting apart."

"Don't be so silly!" he exclaimed with one of his light, genial laughs. "Our life is very much on track. You're a doer and an achiever, and you have a career you love. You're doing extremely well, and you've accomplished so much with the design studio. I'm going great guns at the law firm. Things couldn't be better on that score. So why do you ask what our life is all about? I don't understand what you mean."

All of a sudden she knew that he didn't, that he was genuinely puzzled. She exclaimed, "But we're never together. We're always in different places, and when we are in the same city, you constantly work late. And when we're at home you haven't got a lot to say to me anymore, Peter; and there's another thing, we don't seem to be as close physically as we were." It was on the tip of her tongue to ask him if he was having an affair, and then she changed her mind. He might well ask her the same question, and then what would she say?

Peter was shaking his head, looking miserable, the laughter of earlier wiped out of his eyes. He threw the ties onto a chair and sat down on the bed next to her, took hold of her hand. "But, Vanessa, I love you, you know that. Nothing's changed. Well, I guess it has. I'm successful, very successful, and in a way I never dreamed I could be. This is the big one for me, the big chance, and I don't want to screw it up. I can't, because what I do now, how I handle everything now, is for our future. Yours and mine. Our old age, you might say."

"Old age!" she exploded. "But I don't care about that! I want to live now, while I'm still young."

"We are living, and living very well. And doing well. That's what counts, sweetie." He gazed into her eyes, and said more softly, "I guess I've been neglecting you lately. I'm sorry." He put his arms around her, tried to kiss her, but Vanessa drew away from him.

"You always think you can solve our problems, our disagreements, by making love to me," she said.

"But you know we always *do* solve what ails us when we're in bed together. We work it out that way."

"Just for once it would be nice to make love with you because we *want* to make love, not to get us over one of our quarrels."

"Then let's do it right now."

"I don't want to, Peter. I'm not in the mood. Sorry, but this little girl doesn't want to play tonight."

He recoiled slightly, startled by her sarcastic tone, and said slowly, "Is this about the baby? Is this what all this talk of drifting apart is about? Is that it, Vanessa?"

"No, it's not."

"I know I've been tough on you about having a baby—" he began and stopped abruptly.

"Yes, you have. You made it perfectly clear that you didn't want children."

"I don't. Well, what I mean is, I don't right now. But listen, sweetie, maybe later on, a few years down the line; maybe we can have a child then."

She shook her head and before she could stop herself she said, "Perhaps we ought to separate, Peter. Get a divorce."

His expression changed immediately and he sat up straighter on the bed. "Absolutely not! I don't want a divorce and neither do you. This is silly talk. You're just tired after all the work you did in Venice, and the schedule you've set for yourself with the new collection."

Vanessa was regarding him intently, and she realized that he was afraid of losing her. She could see the fear in his eyes.

When she remained totally silent, Peter went on swiftly, "I promise you things are going to be different, Vanessa. To be honest, I thought you were happy, excited about your design career. I hadn't realized . . . realized that things weren't right between *us*. You do believe me, don't you?"

"Yes," she murmured wearily. "I believe you, Peter." She got up off the bed, and walked toward the bedroom door. Dismay lodged in her chest. "There's not much for dinner. Shall I make pasta and a salad?"

"Certainly not. I'm going to take you out, sweetie. Shall we go next door to Mr. Chow's?"

Vanessa shook her head. "I don't feel like Chinese food."

"Then we'll go to Neary's pub. Jimmy always gives us such a great welcome, and I know you love it there."

9

Vanessa surveyed the living room of the cottage through newly objective and critical eyes. There were no two ways about it, the room looked shabby and decidedly neglected.

She did not care about the shabbiness; the faded wallpaper, the well-washed chintz and worn antique rug were all part of its intrinsic charm. It was the feeling of neglect that bothered her. She knew that the entire cottage was scrupulously clean, since it was maintained by a local woman. But the living room, in particular, had a lackluster air to it.

Bill would be arriving in a few hours to spend the day and part of the next with her, and she wanted the cottage to look nice. Since he spent so much of his time roughing it in battle zones and second-rate hotels, she felt the need to make it comfortable, warm and welcoming for him.

When her parents had divorced several years ago, they had not known what to do with Bedelia cottage. Neither of them had wanted it and yet they had been reluctant to sell it, oddly enough because of sentimental reasons. They both had a soft spot for it.

And so they had ended up giving it to their daughter. Vanessa had been thrilled.

It was located at the far end of Southampton and stood on three acres of land that ran all the way up to the sand dunes and the Atlantic Ocean.

The cottage was not in the chic part of town, nor was it very special, just a simple, stone-and-clapboard house, about forty years old. It had four bedrooms, a large kitchen, a living room, and a library. There was a long, covered veranda at the back of the cottage which fronted onto the sea.

Once the house was hers, she had turned the old red barn into a design studio and office and converted the stone stables into a small foundry with a kiln. It was here in the studio and foundry that she spent most of her time designing and executing the handblown glass prototypes she took to Venice to be copied and produced in Murano.

Being as preoccupied as she was with work, Vanessa did not give the cottage much attention. Piles of old newspapers and magazines, which she had saved for some reason, were stacked here and there; current books, which she hoped one day to read, were piled on a chest and the floor; and, several large vases of dried flowers, which had looked so spectacular in the summer, had lost their color and were falling apart.

Glancing at her watch, she saw that it was just eight o'clock. Bill was arriving at one. Mavis Glover, who had looked after the cottage for years, usually came at nine.

Suddenly deciding not to wait for her to appear, Vanessa made a beeline for the piles of books, carried them to the library next door and found a place for them all on the bookshelves. For the next hour she worked hard in the living room, discarding newspapers, magazines, and the bedraggled dried flowers.

Finally, standing in the middle of the room and glancing around appraisingly, Vanessa decided she had made a vast improvement. Because the room was no longer cluttered, the furniture was suddenly shown off to advantage. The French country antique pieces stood out. Their dark wood tones were mellow against the white walls and the blue chintz patterned with pink and red tulips, which hung at the windows and covered the sofas and chairs.

Not bad, not bad at all, Vanessa thought, and hurried out to the large family-style kitchen. Last night, when she had arrived, she had put the flowers she had brought from the city into vases; now she carried one of these back to the sitting room. The second one she took upstairs to her bedroom.

This had once been her parents' private sanctuary, and to Vanessa it was the nicest room in the cottage. Certainly it was the largest. It had many windows overlooking the sand dunes and the ocean beyond, and a big stone fireplace was set in one of the end walls.

Entirely decorated in yellow and blue, the room had a cheerful, sunny feeling even on the dullest of days. It was comfortable to the point of luxury.

Hurrying forward, Vanessa put the vase of yellow roses on the coffee table in front of the fire, and then went into the bathroom to take a shower. Once she was made up and dressed she would start on lunch while Mavis cleaned the rest of the cottage.

As she stood under the shower, letting the hot water sluice down over her, Vanessa luxuriated for a moment or two in thoughts of Bill. He had arrived in New York last Friday, December the fifteenth, as he had said he would. That was five days ago now. They had managed to snatch several quick drinks together on Sunday and Monday. He was busy with CNS most of the time; but when he was not, she did not want to intrude on hours he had set aside for his daughter.

"I'll drive out to the Hamptons on Wednesday morning," he had told her over their last drink at the Carlyle. "I can stay over until Thursday, if that's all right with you. How does it sound?"

It had sounded wonderful to her, and her beaming face had been her answer to him.

She could hardly wait to see him, have his arms around her, his mouth on hers. At the mere thought of making love with him, her body started to tingle. She snapped her eyes open and turned off the shower.

No time for fantasizing, she chastised herself, reaching for a towel. Anyway, within the space of a few hours she would have the real thing. They would be together.

Once she was dry, Vanessa dressed quickly, choosing a heavy red sweater to go with her well-washed blue jeans. Since it was a cold day, she put on thick white wool socks and brown penny loafers. Her only jewelry was a pair of gold earrings.

Once she had applied a little makeup and sprayed on perfume, she ran downstairs to prepare lunch for Bill.

He was late.

Vanessa sat in the small library, leafing through *Time* and *Newsweek,* wondering where he was, hoping he was not trapped in traffic.

Foolish idea that is, she thought. It was a Wednesday morning in the middle of December, and the traffic had to be light from Manhattan. It was only in the summer that it became a nightmare. She was quite certain Bill would find it straight sailing today; she had given him explicit driving instructions, and, anyway, the cottage was easy to find, just off the main road.

By one forty-five, when he had still not arrived, her anxiety was growing more acute by the minute. She was just deciding whether or not to call the network when she heard a car drawing up outside and she rushed to the front door.

When she saw Bill alighting, then taking his bag out of the trunk, she felt weak with relief. A moment later he was walking into the house, his face wreathed in smiles.

He took hold of her at once, pulled her into his arms. She clung to him tightly.

"Sorry, darling," he said against her hair. "I was delayed at the network and then it was tough getting out of New York this morning. A lot of traffic. Christmas shoppers, I guess."

"It's all right . . . I thought something had happened to you."

"Nothing's going to happen to me," he said, tilting her face to his in that special way he had.

"Let's go into the living room. It's warmer," Vanessa murmured, taking his arm. "I've got white wine on ice, or would you prefer scotch?"

"White wine's fine, thanks."

They stood together in front of the roaring fire, sipping their wine and staring at each other over the rims of their glasses.

"I've missed you, Vanessa."

"I've missed you too."

"You know something . . . I think about you all the time."

"So do I—I think of you, I mean."

"It's funny," he said softly, looking at her closely. "I feel as if you've been in my life always, as if I've known you always."

"Yes. It's the same for me, Bill."

He shook his head, smiled faintly. "I didn't dare touch you when we were in the bar of the Carlyle . . . you're very inflammatory to me."

She stared at him, saying nothing.

He stared back.

Putting his glass on the mantelpiece, he then did the same with hers, moved closer to her, and brought her into the circle of his arms. He kissed her hard, pressing her even closer to him, wanting her to know how much she excited him.

Vanessa tightened her embrace, responding to him with ardor, and this further inflamed him. Bill said in a low, hoarse voice, "I want you so much, want to be close to you."

Pulling away from him, she nodded, took hold of his hand, and led him upstairs to her bedroom.

There was tremendous tension between them. They undressed with great speed, sharing an urgent need to be intimate and closely joined. As they fell on the bed, his hands were all over her body. Loving hands that touched, stroked, explored, and brought her to a fever pitch of excitement.

They could not get enough of each other. He continued to kiss her, and she returned his kisses with the same intense passion she had felt in Venice. And Bill luxuriated in the nearness of her, in the knowledge that she longed for him, needed him so desperately. He felt the same need for her. It was a deep, insatiable need.

Stretching his body alongside hers, he took her suddenly, moving into her so swiftly he heard her gasp with surprise and pleasure. As she clasped him tightly in her arms, her legs wrapped around him, they shared a mounting joy.

Vanessa lay quietly in his arms.

The wintry afternoon sunshine cast its pale light across the yellow walls, turning them to bosky gold.

The only sound was the light rise and fall of Bill's breath as he drowsed and, far beyond the windows, the faint, distant roar of the Atlantic Ocean.

She found the stillness soothing.

Their lovemaking had been passionate, almost frantic, and even more feverish than in Venice. Their need for each other had been so overwhelming, it had stunned them both; afterward they had stared at each other in astonishment. Now this tranquillity was like a balm.

Stretching her body slightly, trying not to disturb him, Vanessa took pleasure from her sense of satisfaction and fulfillment. How different she was with Bill; she even surprised herself. Each time they made love, they seemed to soar higher and higher, reach a greater pitch of ecstasy. It always left her reeling.

In some ways, Vanessa no longer recognized herself. She knew she had undergone a vast change since meeting Bill Fitzgerald. He brought out something erotic and sensual in her, made her feel whole, very feminine, very much a woman.

Pushing herself up onto one elbow, Vanessa looked down at him. The tense, worried expression he invariably wore had disappeared. In repose, his face was smooth, free of pain and concern. He looked so young, very vulnerable. And he touched her deeply.

Vanessa was aware that they had an intimacy of heart and mind as well as body, and it pleased her. They genuinely understood each other, and this compatibility gave them a special kind of closeness that few people shared.

She knew she was in love with him. She knew she wanted to be with him. For always. But was that possible? How could it be? She was not free. She had a husband who loved her, who was terrified of losing her. And for her part, she owed him loyalty and consideration.

Troubling thoughts of Peter insinuated themselves into her mind. She pushed them to one side. Too soon to think of the future . . . Later. She would think about it later.

In the meantime, she was absolutely certain of one thing. With Bill Fitzgerald she was her true self, without pretense or artifice. She was the real Vanessa Stewart.

She brought a tray of food and a bottle of white wine upstairs to the bedroom, where they had a picnic in front of the fire. And after they had devoured smoked salmon sandwiches, Brie cheese and apples, and downed a glass of wine each, they dressed and went out.

The thin sun still shone in the pale azure sky and the Atlantic had the gleam of silver on it. It was a blustery day with a high wind whipping the waves to turbulence.

Bundled up in overcoats and scarves, their arms

wrapped around each other, they walked along the dunes, oblivious to the world, to everything except themselves and their intense feelings for each other.

At one moment Bill stopped and spun her to face him, looked down into her expressive gray eyes. "I'm so happy!" he exclaimed. "Happier than I've been for years."

"What did you say?" she shouted back, also competing with the roar of the ocean.

". . . happier than I've been for years," he repeated, grinning at her, catching her around her waist, pulling her to him. "I love you," he said, his mouth on her ear. "I love you, Vanessa Stewart."

"And I love you, Bill Fitzgerald."

"I didn't hear you," he teased.

"I LOVE YOU, BILL FITZGERALD!" she screamed at the top of her lungs.

His joyous laughter filled the air.

She joined in his laughter, hugging him to her.

And then, holding hands, they ran along the sand dunes, buffeted forward by the wind, euphoric in their love, happy to be alive, to be together.

Later that evening they sat in front of the fire in her bedroom, listening to Mozart's violin concertos.

Vanessa, suddenly looking across at Bill, saw how

preoccupied he was as he stared into the flames, noted how tensely set his shoulders were.

"Are you all right?" she asked in a soft voice. When he did not respond, she pressed, "Bill, is something wrong?"

He lifted his head, looking directly at her. But still he said nothing. Disturbed by the sadness on his face, she went on, "Darling, what is it? You look so . . . unhappy . . . even troubled."

He took a moment, averting his eyes, focusing again on the fire. Finally he said, "This is not a game for me."

Frowning, she gaped at him. "It isn't a game for me either."

Bill said, "This afternoon I told you I loved you. It's the truth."

There was such a questioning look on his face she couldn't help but exclaim, "And I love you. I *meant* what I said, Bill. I don't lie. Do you doubt me?"

He was silent.

"How could you possibly doubt me?" she cried, her voice rising. "It's not possible to simulate the kind of emotions you and I have been sharing since we met."

"I know that, and don't misunderstand my silence," he was quick to answer. "I know you have deep feelings for me." Leaning forward, he took hold of her hand, gripped it in his. "I just want you to know that I'm serious about you—" He paused, pinned his eyes on her. "I'm playing for keeps."

Vanessa nodded.

"Just so long as you know," he said.

"Yes, I do, Bill."

"I'll never let you go, Vanessa."

"You might change your mind," she began, but halted when she saw the stern expression on his face.

"I won't."

Vanessa sat back on the sofa, gazed abstractedly at the painting above the fireplace.

He asked in a low voice, "What are you going to do?"

"I'll tell Peter I want a divorce."

"Are you sure?"

"Yes, I'm sure."

"So am I. I've never been more sure of anything in my life." Moving closer to her on the sofa, he put his arms around her and held her against him. And he knew he had the world in his arms. She was the only woman for him, the only woman he wanted.

10

Bill had asked Vanessa to meet him at Tavern On The Green at twelve-thirty on Saturday, and as she walked into the famous restaurant in Central Park she realized what a good choice it had been.

Always festive at any time of year, it was spectacular during the Christmas season. Beautifully decorated Christmas trees were strategically placed, strings of tiny fairy lights were hung in festoons throughout while branches of holly berries in vases and pink and red poinsettias in wooden tubs added an extra fillip to the seasonal setting.

The magnificent Venetian glass chandeliers, which were permanent fixtures in the main dining room, seemed more appropriate than ever at this time of year.

Bill spotted her immediately. Rising, he left the table and hurried forward to meet her.

As he came toward her, she thought how handsome he looked, and he was extremely well-dressed today. He wore a navy blue blazer, blue shirt, navy tie, and gray pants. He was bandbox perfect, right down to his well-polished brown loafers.

Grabbing her hands, he leaned into her, murmured, "You look great, darling," and gave her a perfunctory kiss on the cheek. "Come and meet the other two women I love," he added as he led her to the table, the proud smile still in place.

Vanessa saw at once how attractive and elegant his mother was, and she seemed much younger than sixty-two. Dressed in a dark red wool suit that set off her beautifully coiffed auburn hair, she looked more like Bill's older sister than his mother.

Sitting next to his mother was undoubtedly the most exquisite child Vanessa had ever seen. She had delicate, perfectly sculpted features, wide-set cornflower blue eyes that mirrored Bill's, and glossy dark blonde hair that fell in waves and curls to her shoulders.

"I've never seen a child who looks like that," Vanessa exclaimed softly, turning to Bill. "Helena's . . . why she's positively breathtaking."

He squeezed her arm. "Thank you, and yes, she is lovely looking, even though I say so myself."

They came to a standstill at the table, and Bill said, "Mom, I'd like to introduce Vanessa Stewart. And Vanessa, this is my mother, Drucilla."

"I'm so glad to meet you, Mrs. Fitzgerald," Vanessa said, taking his mother's outstretched hand.

"Hello, Miss Stewart." Drucilla smiled at her warmly.

"Oh, Mrs. Fitzgerald, please call me Vanessa."

"Only if you call me Dru, everyone does."

"All right, I will. Thank you." Vanessa looked down at the little girl dressed in a blue wool dress, who was observing her with enormous curiosity. "And you must be Helena," she said, offering the six-year-old her hand.

"Yes, I am," Helena said solemnly, taking her hand.

"This is Vanessa," Bill said.

"I'm delighted to meet you, Helena," Vanessa murmured, and seated herself in the chair Bill had pulled out for her.

"Now, what shall we have to drink?" Bill asked, looking at all of them. "How about champagne?"

"That would be nice," Vanessa said.

"Yes, it would, Bill," his mother agreed.

"Is this a celebration?" Helena asked, gazing up at Bill, her head on one side.

"Why do you ask that, Pumpkin?"

"Gran says champagne is only for celebrations."

"Then it's a celebration," Bill responded, his love for his child spilling out of his eyes.

"And what's this celebration?" Helena probed.

Bill thought for a moment, looked at his mother, and answered, "Being here together, the four of us. Yes, that's what we're celebrating, and Christmas, too, of course."

"But I'm not allowed champagne," Helena remarked, staring at him, then swiveling her eyes to Dru. "Am I, Gran?"

"Certainly not," her grandmother responded firmly. "Not until you're grown up."

Bill said, "But you are allowed a Shirley Temple, and that's what I'm going to order for you right now." As he was speaking, Bill signaled to a hovering waiter, who promptly came over to the table and took the order.

Vanessa said to Dru, "It was a great idea of Bill's to suggest coming here for lunch; it's such a festive place."

Dru nodded. "You're right, it's fabulous. Bill tells me you met in Venice. When he was there with Frank Peterson."

"Yes . . ." Vanessa hesitated and then, noticing Bill's beaming face, she went on more confidently, "We spent Thanksgiving together."

"The only three Americans in Venice on that particular day," Bill interjected. "So we had no alternative but to celebrate together. And a good time was had by all."

"I'd like to go to Venice," Helena announced, looking from her father to her grandmother. "Can I?"

"One day, sweetheart," Bill said. "We'll take you when you're a bit older."

"Do you work with my daddy?" Helena asked, zeroing in on Vanessa.

"No, I don't," Vanessa answered. "I'm not in television, Helena. I'm a glass designer."

The child's smooth brow furrowed. "What's that?"

"I design objects, lovely things for the home, which are made in glass. In Venice."

"Oh."

Vanessa had been carrying a small shopping bag when she arrived, and this she had placed with her handbag on the floor. Now she reached for it, took out a gift tied with a large pink bow, and announced, "This is for you, Helena."

The child took it, held it in her hands, staring at the prettily wrapped present. "What is it?"

"Something I made for you."

"Can I open it now, Daddy?"

"Yes, but what do you say first?"

"Thank you, Vanessa." Helena untied the ribbon, took off the paper, and then lifted the lid off the box.

"It's quite fragile," Vanessa warned. "Lift it out of the tissue paper gently."

Helena did as she was bidden, held the glass object in her hands carefully, her eyes wide. It was a twisted, tubular prism that narrowed to a point. Its facets caught and held the light, reflecting the colors of the rainbow. "Oh, it's beautiful," the child gasped in delight.

"It's an icicle. An icicle of many colors, and I made it specially for you, Helena."

"Thank you," Helena repeated, continuing to hold the icicle, moving it so that the glass caught the light.

"It is very beautiful," Dru murmured, turning to Vanessa. "You're a very talented artist."

"Thank you."

Bill said, "May I look at it, Helena?"

"Yes, Dad. Be careful. Vanessa says it's fragile."

"I will," he murmured, his eyes smiling at Vanessa as he took the icicle. "This is quite wonderful," he said, and then nodded when the waiter brought the champagne in a bucket of ice. "You can open it now, please," he said.

After the glass icicle was returned to its box and put on the floor next to Helena's chair, and the wine had been poured, Bill lifted his flute. "Happy Christmas, everyone."

"Happy Christmas," they all responded.

Helena took a sip of her Shirley Temple and put it

down on the table. Turning, she stared hard at Vanessa, and, with undisguised inquisitiveness, she asked, "Are you Daddy's girlfriend?"

Taken aback by the child's candor, Vanessa was speechless for a moment.

Bill answered for her. "Yes, she is, Helena." He smiled at his little daughter, then looked over her head at his mother, raising a brow eloquently.

Drucilla Fitzgerald nodded her approval. And she did approve of this pretty young woman whom she had known for only twenty minutes. There was something about Vanessa that was special; she could tell that, being the good judge of character that she was. Vanessa was to be encouraged, Dru decided. Anyone who could bring this look of happiness to her son's face had her vote of confidence. He had been so lonely after Sylvie's death. And morose for years. She had not seen him so buoyant, spirited, and full of good cheer for the longest time. Suddenly, she felt as if a weight had been lifted off her shoulders.

"Let's order lunch," Bill said. "Do you know what you want, Pumpkin?"

"Yes, Daddy. I'd like to have eggs with the muffin, like we did last time."

"Eggs Benedict," Dru clarified. "I'd love it too, but I don't think I'd better. Not with my cholesterol. I suppose I'll have to settle for crab cakes."

Bill looked at Vanessa. "Do you know what you want?"

"I'll have the same as your mother, Bill, thank you."

"And I'll keep Helena company, go for the Eggs Benedict," he said.

Helena touched Vanessa's arm. "Are you going to marry Daddy?"

Vanessa was further startled by the child's outspoken question, and by her precocity. She glanced swiftly at Bill.

Dru sat back in her chair, observing the three of them.

Bill grinned at Helena and said, "You ask too many questions, Pumpkin, just like Uncle Frank does sometimes. And we don't know yet whether we're going to get married or not ... we need to spend more time together, get to know each other better."

Helena nodded.

Bill went on, "But you and Gran will be the first to know if we do. I promise you."

Later, as Bill helped Vanessa into a cab, he whispered, "Not a bad idea my kid had, eh?"

"Not a bad idea at all," Vanessa replied.

"Take this, darling," he said, pressing something into her hand.

"What is it?" she asked, looking down at it, realizing that it was a key. "What's this for?"

"The suite I booked at the Plaza. For us. Suite 902. Can we meet for a drink later tonight? Say around nine?"

"But of course," she said and slipped the key into her bag.

11

VENICE, JANUARY 1996

It had been raining all afternoon, hard, driving rain that was still coming down in an endless stream. The sky was the color of anthracite, pitted here and there with threatening black clouds, and below her the Grand Canal was swollen, looked as if it might overflow at any moment.

Vanessa turned away from the window and moved into the room, shivering slightly. Although Bill had turned up the heat earlier, when she had first arrived from the airport there had been a chill in the air. It was a dampness that seemed to permeate her bones. She tightened the belt on the bathrobe she was wearing and shrugged further into it as she huddled in a chair near the radiator.

Vanessa was glad to be back in Venice with Bill. It was the first time they had seen each other since Christmas. He had left New York at the end of December, to travel through the Middle East and Europe. Tel Aviv, Jerusalem, Amman, Beirut, Ankara, and Athens were some of the cities on his list. He was busy preparing his special on international terrorism for CNS; time was of the essence since it had been scheduled to air early in March.

Bill had arrived at the Gritti Palace a day earlier than Vanessa, flying in from Athens the night before just as she was leaving New York. They would have five days together in their favorite city. She had work to do out at the glass foundry on Murano. Bill was going to polish his script for the show, and they would be together in the afternoons and evenings.

A smile touched her mouth as she thought of Bill and her love for him. He meant more to her than she had ever imagined possible. He was the man of her life. For the rest of her life. They were meant to be together, and there was nothing that could keep them apart. She knew that now.

A small sigh escaped as she thought of the past few weeks. Apart from seeing Bill, meeting his mother and Helena, December had been a ghastly month for her. Peter had stayed in London longer than he had intended, and after his return to Manhattan he had left almost immediately for Los Angeles. He had been away so much she had barely had a chance to discuss their private life, and Christmas had been miserable for the most part.

Finally, early in January, she had cornered him one evening when he returned from the office earlier than usual. Endeavoring to be as gentle as possible, while displaying no weakness whatsoever, Vanessa had told him she wanted a divorce.

Peter had reacted badly, overreacted really, and had been adamant that they remain married. Even though he had agreed, in the end, that their relationship was no longer what it had once been, he nonetheless refused even to consider divorcing. Very simply, he balked at the idea and wouldn't listen to her. At least not that particular evening.

Vanessa had come to realize that there was only one thing to do, and that was to get on with her life, lead it as she saw fit, and be independent. Ten days before leaving on this trip to Venice, she had taken her courage in both hands and left Peter, moving all of her clothes and possessions into the loft in Soho.

The loft had once been an apartment before she had turned it into a studio-office, and it had a good-sized working kitchen, a full bathroom, plus a guest toilet. Once she had purchased a sofa bed and installed it in the back storage room, turning this into a bedroom, the loft had become a comfortable place to live. Most important, it had made Peter realize just how determined she was to end their marriage. Her departure had a tremendous impact on him; he at last understood how serious she was about a divorce.

As her mother had said to her, "Actions make more of a statement than words ever could, Vanny, and it's best to end this now, while you're both still young enough to start all over again, find new partners." Both of her parents had been very supportive of her decision to leave Peter. However, she had not told them about Bill, deeming it wiser to keep her own counsel at this moment.

Vanessa heard Bill's key in the lock and glanced at the door as he came in. Getting up, she went to him, her face full of smiles.

He had gone downstairs a few minutes earlier to pick up a fax which had arrived from New York. Now he waved it and said, "Neil Gooden and Jack Clayton *love* the footage so far. Neil says he can't wait to see the rest of it." Bill handed her the fax. "Here, read it yourself, darling."

She scanned the two pages, digested everything, and handed it back to him. "Congratulations, Bill. From what Neil says, you've worked miracles and in less than three weeks. Aren't you thrilled he thinks it's going to be a smash?"

"From his mouth to God's ears," Bill said with a huge grin, and putting his arm around her shoulders he walked her over to the sofa.

"I do think it's coming together, though. I just need

to cover two more cities and then it's a wrap, as far as the field reporting is concerned. When you go back to New York, I'll head for Paris, work there a couple of days with my crew and the producer. Then we'll all go on to Northern Ireland, make Belfast our last stop. Incidentally, I've finally come up with a good title."

"What is it?"

"I'm thinking of calling the special *Terrorism: The Face of Evil*. What's your feeling about it?"

"I think it sounds good. And it says exactly what you mean."

He nodded. "Yes, I guess it does. What I've managed to do is cover terrorism around the world. I've been filming interviews with experts, and some terrorists who are in jail in Israel. I'm backing up the new stuff with footage of past acts of terrorism, from the 1972 killing of the Olympic athletes and Lord Mountbatten's murder by the IRA to the Lockerbie crash, the World Trade Center bombing, and the Oklahoma City explosion. I've endeavored to make it very personal, very intimate. I want it to hit home, touch the average American. I'll be using some interviews I did with survivors of terrorism, and relatives of victims of terrorists. I'm quite gratified by the way it's come together." Bill got up, walked across to the mini bar, and took a bottle of mineral water from it. "Do you want anything, Vanessa?"

She shook her head.

Bill strode back to the sofa, sat down next to her. After taking a sip of water, he placed the bottle on the coffee table and placed his arm around her. "Moving into the loft was a very good idea, Vanessa. It's shown Peter how serious you are about a divorce."

"Yes, it has. He phoned me yesterday, just as I was leaving for Kennedy. And while he didn't actually *agree* to a divorce, he did sound more amenable, if a little crushed. I have the feeling he's beginning to accept the idea."

"That's a relief." Bill looked at her intently. "Did you tell him about me? About us?"

"No, I didn't, Bill. I didn't think it was necessary. And anyway, it would be like a red flag to a bull. Very inflammatory."

"I don't care if he knows, you know. I'm a big boy. I can look after myself."

"Yes, but why rub salt in the wound? Anyway, Peter really has come to accept how bad our relationship has been for the last few years . . . I prefer to leave it at that."

"Whatever you say, sweetheart, you're the boss."

She gave him the benefit of a loving smile.

He leaned closer, kissed her on the mouth. "The concierge just told me Venice will be flooded by seven o'clock. No Harry's Bar tonight, I'm afraid. We'll have to eat here."

"That's fine, Bill. The restaurant downstairs is good."

"Oh, but I thought we would have room service, eat here in the suite."

"Yes, if you want, I think it's more comfortable anyway, and I don't have to get dressed."

He nodded and reached for her. "My thought precisely."

"You once suggested that we make Venice our point of rendezvous," Bill said to her much later that evening, after they had made love, eaten dinner, and made love again. "And I think that's a great idea. It's going to be very convenient for me."

They were in bed and Vanessa lay within the circle of his arms. She swiveled her eyes to meet his. "What do you mean?"

"When I've finished the special on terrorism, I'm being assigned to the Middle East. I'll be based either in Israel or Lebanon, that's up to me. But whichever it is, I can fly straight up to Venice. It's an easy trip. I'll try to be here whenever you're working at the foundry in Murano, if only for a couple of days, or a long weekend."

Her face lit up. "Oh, Bill, that'll be wonderful, being able to see you every month. Well, more or less. Why the Middle East, though?"

"I didn't want to go back to Bosnia, as you know, even though there's trouble there again. There always will be, too, if you ask me. And the peace accords are very fragile, not likely to last, especially if the UN troops leave. Still, I wanted out, and Jack Clayton was aware of that ages ago. So he asked me if I'd like to go back to the Middle East to cover the whole area. I know it well, and Frankie's in Lebanon. So it'll be like old home week." He grinned at her. "As I'm telling you this, I'm beginning to realize that I will base myself in Beirut, set up camp with Frankie at the Commodore Hotel."

"When will that be, darling?"

"In March sometime. I'll be cutting and editing at CNS in New York in the middle of February, preparing the special. And then I'll go."

"I thought everything was quiet in the Middle East right now."

"As quiet as that area will ever be. There are always rumblings of some kind, somewhere, be it Iran, Libya, Saudi Arabia, Syria, Israel, or Iraq. You name it. Flare-ups happen all the time," Bill explained.

"If your assignment starts in March, when do you think we can meet here again?"

Bill held her closer, smiling at her, his blue eyes crinkling at the corners. "In March, of course. The end of March."

12

"Are you sure there are no messages for me?" Vanessa said, her eyes focused intently on the concierge standing behind the desk at the Gritti Palace.

"No, Signora Stewart, no messages." His faint smile seemed almost apologetic as he added, "No, nothing at all. No faxes, nothing, signora."

"Thank you." Vanessa turned away from the desk and walked rapidly toward the elevator.

Once she was back in her room, she sat down at the writing table in front of the window and gazed absently out at the Grand Canal.

It was a cool, breezy Saturday in late March, but the sun had come out and given a certain radiance to the afternoon. Yet she was hardly aware of the weather; her thoughts were focused on Bill. She opened her appointment book and stared at the date. It was March the thirtieth, and she had been in Venice for four days, working at the foundry on Murano. Bill was supposed to have arrived on Thursday afternoon, the twenty-eighth, to join her for a long weekend.

But he was forty-eight hours late, and she did not understand why. After all, it was not as if he were in a war zone and in any danger. Beirut was quiet at the moment; he had told her that himself. She dismissed the idea that something might have happened to him.

It struck her then that he could have gone somewhere else in the Middle East to cover a story. He had talked about Egypt and the Sudan to her when he had been in New York in February. They had been able to meet only once at that time because he had been busy editing his special on terrorism, and then he had had to leave for Beirut.

Yes, that was most likely the reason he was late. Right now he was probably on a plane, flying to Venice from some distant spot. This thought cheered her, but an instant later she was worrying again. If he had been delayed because he was caught up on a story, why hadn't he phoned her?

Frowning to herself, Vanessa reached for her address book and quickly found the number of the Commodore Hotel in Beirut. Glancing at the hotel's chart for direct dialing to foreign cities, she picked up the phone and punched in the numbers for Beirut and the hotel.

It was only a second or two before she heard the hotel operator saying, "Hotel Commodore."

"Mr. Bill Fitzgerald, please."

"Just a moment, please."

She heard the ringing tone. It seemed to her to be interminable. He did not pick up. He was not in his room.

"There's no answer," the operator said. "Do you wish to leave a message?"

"Yes. Please say Vanessa Stewart called. He can reach me at the Gritti Palace in Venice." She then gave the operator the number and hung up, sat staring at the phone.

After a few moments, she rose and walked over to the coffee table. Picking up the remote control, she turned up the volume on the television set. The CNS weatherman was giving the weekend forecast for the States. She sat down on the bed and watched CNS for the next couple of hours.

World news. American news. Business news. Sports news. But no news of Bill Fitzgerald, chief foreign correspondent for CNS.

Later in the evening, for the umpteenth time that day, Vanessa checked her answering machines at the Manhattan loft and the cottage in Southampton. There was no message from Bill.

At one point she ordered sandwiches, fruit, and a pot of hot tea. She had not eaten anything since breakfast, and suddenly she was feeling hungry. After her light supper she watched CNS until the early hours, although she did so with only half an eye. It was mostly repeats of everything she had seen earlier, and her mind was elsewhere anyway.

On Sunday morning, after she had drunk a quick cup of coffee, Vanessa dialed the Commodore Hotel in Beirut and asked for Bill Fitzgerald.

Once again, there was no answer in his room.

This time, Vanessa asked to be put through to Frank Peterson. She clutched the phone tightly, listening to the ring, hoping that at least Frank would pick up. He did not.

After a split second the hotel operator was back on the line. "I'm sorry, both of them seem to be out, miss. Would you like to leave a message?"

"Yes, for Mr. Fitzgerald. Please ask him to call Vanessa Stewart at the Gritti Palace in Venice."

Vanessa spent a miserable Sunday, waiting for the phone to ring and watching CNS and CNN on television, alternating between the two cable networks. At one point she checked her answering machines in the States, but there were no messages. Not a whisper from anyone. She even phoned the international news desk at CNS headquarters in New York. But they wouldn't give her any information about Bill's whereabouts.

By late afternoon she had given up hope of Bill arriving. In any case, she was due to leave for New York on Monday morning, and so she got out her suitcase and began to pack. She did so in a flurry of emotions —frustration, anger, disappointment, worry, and dismay.

That night, when she went to bed, Vanessa was unable to sleep. She turned restlessly for hours, praying for morning to come.

Eventually she must have dozed off because she awakened with a start as dawn was breaking. As she lay there in the dim, gray light Vanessa finally acknowledged what she had been denying all weekend: The real reason Bill had not shown up was because he was no longer interested in her. Their affair was over for him. Finished. Dead.

No, she thought, he cared too much. I'm wrong.

And yet deep down she knew she was right. There was no other possible reason for his absence.

She closed her eyes, remembering all the things he had said to her . . . that he loved her . . . that he was playing for keeps . . . that he was serious about her . . . that this wasn't a game for him. He'd even encouraged her to divorce Peter. Why did he do that, if he hadn't meant what he said?

Well, of course he meant those things when he said them, that niggling voice at the back of her head muttered. He was glib, slick, smooth. A wordsmith. Clever with all those wonderful words that tripped off his tongue so lightly. Wasn't that all part of his talent? Hadn't he told her that his grandmother had always said, when he was growing up, that he'd kissed the Blarney Stone?

There was another thing, too. He was back in the close company of Frank Peterson, his best friend, his alter ego. Frank was a man Bill had characterized as a womanizer with a terminal Don Juan complex. Those had been his exact words. Maybe they were off somewhere together for the weekend. Bill was very close to Frank, and impressed by him. And perhaps some of Frank's habits were contagious.

Suddenly she felt like a fool. She had been sitting here waiting for Bill for four days and there hadn't been the slightest word from him. As chief foreign correspondent for CNS he had access to phones wherever he was. He could have called her from anywhere.

But he had not, and that was a fact she could not ignore.

Dismay lodged in the pit of her stomach and she found herself trembling. Tears sprang into her eyes and she sat up, brushing them aside as she turned on the light, looked at her travel clock. It was five o'clock. She sat on the side of the bed for a moment, endeavoring to pull herself together. As painful as it was, she had to admit that she had been dumped. Why, she would never know. She began to cry again, and she discovered that she could not stop.

13

"Over the years, I've discovered that the more you love a person, the more they're bound to disappoint you in the end," her mother had once said to her, adding: "And, in my opinion, men understand this better than we do. That's why they rather cleverly spread their bets. Always remember that, Vanny. Don't give all for love. And don't be duped."

But she had given all for love. And she had been duped. And she had remembered her mother's wise words far too late for them to matter.

Was it true? Did men spread their bets when it came to women? Was that what Bill had done?

Certainly she had loved him a lot, put all of her trust in him. And in the end he *had* bitterly disappointed her. But no, wait, it was so much more than disappointment, wasn't it? He had humiliated her, made her feel foolish, even ridiculous, and he had hurt her so badly she thought she would never recover from that hurt. It cut deep . . . deep into her very soul.

She had been so open with him, so honest, baring her soul, her innermost secret self. She had given him everything she had to give, far more than she had given any other man, even her husband.

Seemingly, her gifts of love and adoration had meant nothing to him. He had discarded her as easily as he had picked her up in the bar of the Hotel Gritti Palace.

Unexpectedly, and quite suddenly, she remembered something he had said to her about Frank, something about Frank hedging his bets as far as women were concerned. Perhaps all men did that.

Vanessa let out a long sigh and walked on across the sand dunes, her heart heavy, her mind still fogged by the pain of Bill's defection.

It was a fine, clear day in the middle of April—cold, with a pale sun in a pale sky. The Atlantic Ocean was calmer than it had been for days despite the wind that was blowing up.

She lifted her eyes and stared up into the sky when she heard the *cawk-cawk* of seagulls. She watched them as they wheeled and turned against the clouds.

The wind buffeted her, driving her toward the beach. She hunched down farther into her heavy duffle coat and stuck her gloved hands into her pockets. She felt dispirited to the point of depression.

She was well aware that her depressed emotional state was because of Bill Fitzgerald and what he had done to her. She found it hard to believe that he had disappeared from her life in the way that he had, but it was true. At times she even tried to tell herself she didn't care. But of course she did.

Their love affair had been so intense, so sexual, so passionate in every way and so . . . *fierce.* He had swept her off her feet and into his bed and then out of his life when he had grown tired of her. Just like that. *Puff!* She was gone. Had their affair been too hot? Had it burned out too fast for him? She was not sure. How could she be sure . . . of anything . . . ever again?

Vanessa felt the splatter of raindrops on her face and immediately looked up. Thunderheads were darkening that etiolated sky, turning it to leaden gray, and there was the sudden bright flourish of lightning, then the crack of thunder.

Turning swiftly, she walked back to the cottage at the edge of the dunes. She made it just in time. It was a cloudburst. The heavens opened and the rain poured down.

She locked the door behind her, took off her duffle, and went into the library. Here she turned on lamps, struck a match, and brought the flame to the paper and logs Mavis had stacked in the grate.

Since she had returned, Mavis Glover had taken to coming almost every day, fussing over her, bringing her fruit and vegetables and other groceries. Once Mavis had even offered to pick up newspapers and magazines, but Vanessa had told her not to bother. She was not interested in the outside world; she had cut herself off from it.

She had returned from Venice and moved out to Southampton permanently. She had turned herself into a virtual hermit. She had unplugged her telephone and pulled the plugs on the radio and the television. In fact, she vowed she would never look at television again as long as she lived.

She was out of contact with everyone. Out of action. The only person she saw or spoke to was Mavis.

Licking my wounds, she thought now as she sank onto the sofa in front of the fire. Licking my wounds like a sick animal.

The truth was, she did not want to see anyone, not even her mother. The world was well lost for her.

Peter had sent the divorce papers; they had arrived yesterday by special delivery. She had laughed loudly and hollowly when she had seen them. As if they mattered now. She had pushed for the divorce when Bill was a part of her life, and now seemingly he had discarded her.

The anger flared again in her and with it came the hot, endless tears. Pushing her face down into the cushions, she cried until she thought there were no tears left in her.

She sat up with a start. The fire had almost gone out. Glancing at the mantelpiece, she focused on the clock. It was just five. Time to go to work.

Pushing herself up off the sofa, Vanessa looked out of the window and saw that the rain had ceased. The late afternoon sky, washed clean of the dark clouds, was clear again.

After putting on her duffle coat, she walked slowly across the lawn to the red barn, then stopped for a brief moment as she passed the small copse of trees to the left of the house. Years ago her mother had planted hundreds of daffodils, and she had added to them since she had owned the cottage.

Many of them were pushing their golden heads upward, fluttering in the breeze, pale yellow beacons in the soft light. How fresh and springlike they looked. So pretty under the trees. Her eyes filled. She brushed her damp cheeks with her fingertips and walked on.

Once she was inside her studio, Vanessa focused on her work. Going to the drawing board, she switched on the light above it and was soon sketching rapidly, drawing spheres and globes, until she found her way through the many shapes springing into her mind. She settled, at last, on kidney and oval shapes.

Her work had become her salvation. She found it hard to sleep at night, and so she had reversed her routine. From five o'clock until eleven she created her designs in the barn. She had a drink and ate dinner at midnight, and then read half the night, until fatigue finally overcame her.

And once the designs on paper were finished, she worked in the foundry, hand-blowing the glass pieces. As she did she would ask herself how she would ever be able to go to Venice again. She would have to because of her work. But she knew she must find another hotel. She would never again set foot in the Gritti Palace.

14

"You were *there*, Joe! What really happened?" Frank Peterson exclaimed, his voice rising slightly. His face was pale, and he looked strained and anxious.

Leaning over the table, he pinned his eyes on Joe Alonzo. "What the hell happened to Bill?" he demanded again.

Joe shook his head. He looked as if he were about to burst into tears. "I'm telling you, Frank, it was over before I could blink. We were in West Beirut, not too far from here, near the mosque. We all got out of the car, Mike, Bill, and me. Bill started to walk toward the mosque; Mike and I went to the trunk, to take out our equipment. Suddenly this big Mercedes slid to a stop. Three young men jumped out, grabbed Bill, and hustled him into the car. Then the Mercedes sped off."

"And you didn't follow it!" Frank said in a hard, tight voice, staring at the CNS soundman. "Jesus, Joe!"

"I know, I know, Frank, I can guess what you're

thinking. But the point is, Mike and I were stunned for a second. We couldn't believe it."

"And so you didn't react."

"We did, but not fast enough! Within a few seconds we ran to our car, raced after the Mercedes, but we couldn't find it. The damned thing had just disappeared. Literally, into thin air."

"These local terrorists know all the side streets and back alleys," Frank said, and eyed Joe thoughtfully. "And if you and Mike hadn't been taking your equipment out of the trunk, you would've probably been grabbed as well," he asserted in a quieter tone.

"Damn right we would!" Mike Williams said, coming to a halt at the table where Frank and Joe were sitting in the bar of the Marriott in the Hamra district of Beirut.

Frank jumped up at the sight of Mike, grabbed his hand and shook it. "Join us, Mike, I've just been talking to Joe about Bill's kidnapping."

"It's a hell of a thing . . . we're at our wits' end . . ." Mike sat down heavily. He looked tired and worried. "When did you get back to Beirut, Frank?"

"Last night. From Egypt. I was covering a story there when the new trouble between the Israelis and Hezbollah erupted. The civil war is over, everything's on the mend, and then they start skirmishing again. But did they ever *really* stop?"

"I doubt it," Mike replied. "Still, it's the first time the Israelis have attacked Beirut directly in fourteen years. And with laser-homing Hellfire missiles, no less, shot from four helicopter gunships off the coast. My jaw practically dropped when it happened two days ago."

"Yeah, but the Israelis were actually responding to Hezbollah's bombing of Israel," Joe pointed out quickly.

Frank nodded. "And after Israel's attack on Beirut, Hezbollah retaliated yesterday by sending another forty rockets into Israel. The war of attrition continues."

"Nothing changes much," Mike murmured and motioned to a waiter, ordered scotch on the rocks.

Frank said, "I couldn't believe it when I saw the story on CNS about Bill's kidnapping. My God, I'd just left him when he was taken. I flew out of Beirut on March twenty-seventh and he was grabbed the next day. And for most of the time I was away I thought he was having a good time in Venice."

"He never made it to Venice," Mike responded. "I'm sure you realize the network sat on the story for a few days, hoping he would be released quickly. When he wasn't, they got it on the air at once."

"Who's behind it? Have you heard anything?" Frank probed.

"No, we haven't," Joe answered.

"I was just on the phone to Jack Clayton," Mike

explained. "The network still doesn't have any information. Nobody's claiming this, the way the bastards usually do. It's a bit of a mystery. Total silence from all terrorist groups, according to New York."

"It's got to be Hezbollah," Frank said in a knowing tone. He turned from Mike to Joe, raising a brow. "Who else but them?"

"You're right," Joe agreed. "That's what Mike and I think, too. At least, we believe that the Islamic Jihad is behind it. You know better than anybody, Frank, that the terrorist arm of Hezbollah is full of wackos. They're the ones who took Terry Anderson and William Buckley, and they're not known for fast releases."

"Terry Anderson was a hostage for seven years," Frank muttered.

"Don't remind me," Mike said dourly. "By the way, we've been in touch with Bill's mother."

"I spoke with her myself from Egypt," Frank answered. "As soon as I knew what had happened. It's remarkable the way she's holding up."

Joe volunteered, "We try to call her every few days. Unfortunately, there's not much we can tell her."

"Hearing from you helps her a great deal, I'm sure of that." Frank lifted his glass, downed the last of his scotch. Leaning back in his chair, he thought for a moment about Vanessa. He had tried to reach her for days, but there was no answer at her left or the cottage in the Hamptons. "What's the network doing about trying to find Bill?" he asked.

"There's not a lot they can do," Mike said. "Bill's picture has been circulated throughout Beirut, the whole of Lebanon, in fact. And a great deal of pressure has been put on the Lebanese and Syrian governments, and right from the beginning. Even though the story wasn't released immediately, the CNS top brass were on top of the situation at once, the same day Bill was snatched.

"And pressure was put on the White House as well. Let's face it, Frank, there's nothing anyone can do until an organization claims the kidnapping as theirs. Only then can the U.S. Government and the network start pushing for Bill's release."

"I always kidded him, said he was bulletproof," Frank began and stopped when Allan Brent, the Middle East correspondent for CNN, stopped at their table.

"We've just had a news flash," he said. "Hezbollah is claiming they have Bill Fitzgerald."

"Oh, Jesus!" Frank cried.

"How long ago was the flash?" Joe asked.

Allan Brent glanced at his watch. "It's now seven, about six-thirty, thereabouts."

Mark Lawrence, who was covering Bill's kidnapping

for CNS, appeared in the doorway of the bar. When he spotted the CNS crew with Frank and Allan Brent, he hurried over. He said to Mike, "I guess you've heard that the Islamic Jihad has Bill."

"Yes," Mike said. "Allan just told us."

"I hope to God Bill's all right," Frank cried. "I *pray* to God he's all right. That group is fanatical, unstable, and unpredictable."

It was always dark in the cramped, airless room.

They had nailed old wood boards over the windows and only thin slivers of light crept in through the cracks.

Bill Fitzgerald turned awkwardly on the narrow cot; his movements were restricted by handcuffs and leg chains. Managing at last to get onto his back, he lay staring up at the ceiling, trying to assess what day it was.

All along he had attempted to keep track of time; he figured he had been a hostage for almost two weeks. When he asked his various guards, they wouldn't tell him. All they ever said was, "Shut up, American pig!"

He felt dirty, and wished they would allow him to have another shower. He had only been permitted two since his capture. His clothes had become so filthy he had begged them to give him something clean, which one of his guards had done yesterday. *Finally.* Cotton undershorts, a T-shirt, and a pair of cotton pants had been thrown at him, and he had been unchained in order to change into them. The clothes were cheap, but it was a relief to have them.

He had no idea where he was, whether he was still somewhere in Beirut or in the Bekaa Valley, that hotbed of Hezbollah activities where the Iran-backed militia was in control. So many hostages had been held there.

Bill didn't even know why he had been taken, except that he was an American and a journalist. But he *was* certain of one thing—the identity of his kidnappers. They were young men of the Islamic Jihad, the terrorist arm of Hezbollah, and dangerous. Some of them were slightly crazed, on the edge, capable of anything.

They kept him chained up, shouted abuse at him, beat him every day, and gave him little food or water. And what food they did provide was stale, almost inedible. Yet despite their continuing mistreatment of him, he was not going to let them break his spirit.

Bill kept his mind fully occupied as best he could.

He thought mostly of his child, his mother, and of Vanessa, the woman he loved. He worried about them, worried about how they were reacting to his kidnapping, how they were handling it. He had faith in them, knew they would be strong; even his child would be strong.

As he lay staring at the dirty ceiling, he envisioned Vanessa's face in his mind's eye, projected her image onto the ceiling.

How lovely she was, so special, and so very dear to him. And how lucky he was to have found her. He knew they would have a wonderful life together. The first thing he was going to do when he was free was make a child with her. She wanted one so badly; she had confided that to him the last time they had been together.

He had worried about her for the first few days he was in captivity, knowing she was alone in Venice, waiting for him. And with no idea why he had not shown up.

Bill heard the key turning in the lock. He focused his eyes on the door and steeled himself for his daily beating. In the dim light he saw one of his captors entering the cell.

"Put on blindfold," the young man said, walking across the room, showing the grimy rag to Bill.

"Why?" Bill asked, endeavoring to sit up.

"No speak, American pig! American spy!" the young man shouted and tied the blindfold around Bill's eyes roughly, pulled him to his feet, and led him across the cell.

"Where are you taking me?" Bill demanded.

"No speak!" the terrorist yelled, pushing Bill out of the room.

15

Vanessa sat up with a jerk, feeling disoriented, blinking as she looked around the library. Dimly, in the distance, the thudding noise that had awakened her continued.

She pushed herself to her feet, hurried across the room and out into the hall. Instantly the thudding sounded louder, and she realized that someone was hammering on the front door of the cottage.

She ran across the hall, shouting, "I'm coming," and flung open the door. Much to her surprise and consternation she found herself staring into the face of Bill's mother.

"Dru!" she exclaimed, completely taken aback. "Hello! Have you been knocking long?"

When his mother did not answer, but simply stared at her blankly, Vanessa went on, "Why have you come to see me? What are you doing here?" Her brows knitted together in a frown when suddenly she became aware of Dru Fitzgerald's troubled face and bloodshot eyes. She also noticed that she looked painfully thin. "Dru, what's the matter?" she asked, urgency echoing in her voice.

Dru leaned against the door jamb, unexpectedly breathing hard, as if she was experiencing some sort of difficulty. She managed to say, "May I come inside, Vanessa?"

"How rude of me to keep you standing here. Of course, please come in. Can I get you anything?"

"A glass of water, please. I must take a pill."

Vanessa took hold of Drucilla's arm and escorted her into the cottage. After leading her to the sitting room, and settling her in a chair, she went to the kitchen for the water.

A moment later Vanessa returned. She handed the glass to Dru, waited for her to take the pill, then said, "I can tell you're distressed about something. What's the matter?"

Drucilla Fitzgerald, staring intently at her, realized with a small jolt that Vanessa did not know what had happened to Bill. How that was possible she wasn't sure, but, nonetheless, she was quite certain it was true. Dru wondered how to tell her. Tears flooded her eyes, and she clasped her hands together to stop them from trembling.

Vanessa was about to ask her again what was causing her upset when Dru cleared her throat, reached out and took hold of Vanessa's hand.

Dru said slowly, almost in a whisper, "I've been trying to reach you on the phone for days." No longer able to control herself, she began to weep. She groped in her wool jacket for her handkerchief.

"I've had my phone turned off," Vanessa explained, and as she said these words she had a terrible sense of foreboding. "It's Bill! Something's happened to Bill, hasn't it?"

Dru continued to cry, her sobs almost uncontrollable, her pain even more apparent now.

Vanessa went and sat next to her on the sofa, put her arm around Dru's shoulders. "I'm totally in the dark, Dru. I've had not only the phone turned off but the television as well. I've cut myself off from the world for the past two weeks."

Dru turned to look at her, the tears streaming down her pale face. Her mouth began to tremble. "He's dead," she said in a voice that was barely audible. "My son is dead. My only child has been taken from me in the most cruel way. Oh Vanessa . . . Vanessa . . . Why did they kill him? They shot him. He's never coming back. He's gone. Oh, whatever shall we do without him?" She continued to weep, gasping, holding her arms around her body. Her sorrow was unendurable.

Vanessa was gaping at Dru. She had gone cold all over, and she was stunned, reeling from shock, unable to respond for a moment. Her eyes welled, and she began to shake. At last, she said, "I don't understand . . . *who* killed Bill?" Choking on these words, she was unable to continue, just held onto Dru tightly. The two women clung together, sobbing.

Eventually, through her tears, Dru said, "It was Hezbollah. The Islamic Jihad. They kidnapped Bill, Vanessa. I realize now that you didn't know, otherwise you would have come to Helena and me, to be with us."

"When?" Vanessa gasped. "When was he taken?" Her voice shook and fresh tears flowed; she knew the answer even before Dru spoke.

"March the twenty-eighth," Dru answered. "It was a Thursday. They took him that morning in Beirut. He was out with the crew, Joe and Mike—"

"Oh, my God! My God!" Vanessa cried out, pressing both of her hands to her face, trying to stem the tears. They slid through her fingers, fell down onto her cotton shirt, leaving damp splotches. "I was waiting for him in Venice, and he didn't come! I thought he'd lost interest in me, that it was over between us. But he couldn't come, could he? Oh, Dru, Dru . . ."

"No, he couldn't. He loved you, Vanessa, he wanted to marry you. He told me that. He also told me that you were married, that you were getting a divorce."

Vanessa swallowed hard. "Bill was mine and I was

his and that was the way it was. How could I have forgotten that?"

Drucilla sighed and looked into Vanessa's face sadly. "When we're in love, things are always very extreme, intense . . . "

"I love him with all my heart. I shouldn't ever have doubted him in Venice. I should have known something terrible had happened, something beyond his control."

Dru was silent for a second, and then she said softly, "You were feeling hurt."

Vanessa suddenly lost control again and started to weep bitterly. "When was he shot?" she asked through her tears.

"We're not sure." Dru found it hard to continue. She brought her hand to her trembling mouth, and took a few moments to regain her composure.

Slowly, she went on, "Andrew Bryce, the president of CNS, and Jack Clayton, Bill's news editor, came to see me yesterday." Pausing, she took a deep breath before saying, "To tell me themselves that the Islamic Jihad had just announced they had executed Bill. They left his body at the French Embassy in Beirut, who have given it to the American Hospital to send home."

"But why did they kill him?" Vanessa cried. "*Why,* Dru?"

"Andrew and Jack don't know. No one knows. The Islamic Jihad haven't said anything. They've given no explanation."

The two women who loved Bill Fitzgerald sat together on the sofa, not speaking, lost in their own troubled thoughts, silently sharing their heartbreak and sorrow.

After a while, Vanessa spoke. Looking at Dru, she said, "Where is Helena?"

Dru covered her mouth with her hand once more, the tears starting afresh. After a moment she said, "I brought her with me. I hadn't the heart to leave her. She's walking the dunes with Alice, the nanny. The child's heartbroken, she worshiped him so."

Vanessa nodded. Rising, she walked across the room to the window, stood looking out at the dunes, her mind full of Bill and the love they had shared. She thought of his child. And she came to a sudden decision.

Turning to look at Bill's mother, Vanessa said, "I think you and Helena should stay here with me for a few days, Dru. Bill would want us to be together."

Much later that night, when she was alone in her bedroom, Vanessa wept for Bill once more. She wept for the loss of the man she loved, the life they would never share, and the children they would never have.

It was a long night of tears and anguish. There was a moment when guilt reared up, but she crushed it before it took hold. It was a ridiculous waste of time to feel guilty because she had doubted him briefly. He would be the first to say that, just as his mother had.

As dawn broke over the dunes, Vanessa came to understand that her grief would last for a long time, and that she must let it run its course. Bill Fitzgerald had been the love of her life, and she had lost him in the blink of an eye. Lost him because of some insanity on the other side of the world. It was wrong, all wrong. He had been far too young a man to die.

It should not have happened, but it had, and she was alone. Just as his child and his mother were alone, bereft and lost without him. They were her main concern now. She would do what Bill would want her to do . . . console and comfort them.

They needed her. And she needed them.

16

"I'm glad Alice listened to you, Dru, and took her vacation," Vanessa said, stirring the chicken soup she was making, peering into the pot on the stove. "It would have been foolish of her to cancel it, when she had it all planned. But you know, she never did say where she was going."

Dru did not respond.

Vanessa said, "Where has she gone, actually?"

Still Dru did not answer and Vanessa swung around, exclaimed, "My God, what's wrong," threw down the wooden spoon, and rushed across the kitchen.

Drucilla was leaning back in the chair, her face drained of all color, starkly white against her red hair. She was clutching herself and wincing.

Vanessa bent over her. "Dru, what is it?"

"Pain. In my chest. My left arm hurts. I think I'm having a heart attack."

"Don't move! I'll get the car. Southampton Hospital's not far away. On Meeting House Lane. I'll have us there in a few minutes. Just don't move, Dru. Okay?"

Dru nodded.

Vanessa ran to the garage, backed the car out, parked it near the cottage, and leapt across the lawn to her studio. She had left Helena drawing there earlier. Pulling open the door, she called, "Helena, come on, we have to go!"

"Where?"

"To the hospital. Your grandmother's not well."

"I'm coming," the child shouted fiercely, jumped off the stool, and flew across the floor. "Is it her heart?"

"She thinks so, yes," Vanessa said, took hold of Helena's hand, and ran with her to the cottage. "Get in the car, honey, and I'll be out in a minute with Gran." As she spoke, Vanessa helped Helena into the backseat and fastened the safety belt.

Inside the house, Vanessa grabbed her handbag from the hall closet, and dashed back to the kitchen; Dru was slumped in the chair with her arms still wrapped around herself.

Bending toward her, Vanessa asked, "Dru, do you feel any worse?"

"No. Just the same."

"Can you make it to the car?"

"Yes, Vanessa. If you help me," Dru murmured in a weak voice.

Together the two women walked slowly across the

kitchen and outside to the car. "Try not to worry. You're going to be all right," Vanessa said as she fastened the seat belt around Dru, praying that she would be.

And she kept on praying all the way to the hospital.

"Mrs Fitzgerald *has* had a heart attack, fortunately not too severe," Dr. Paula Matthews said, drawing Vanessa to one side of the waiting room. "She's going to be all right, but she will have to watch herself, take care of herself."

"Yes, I understand, Dr. Matthews, I'll see that she does. In the meantime, how long does she have to be in the hospital?"

"A few days. Five at the most. She's in our cardiac care unit, more for observation and a rest than anything else." The doctor smiled at Vanessa, then glanced at Helena, who was sitting on a chair near the window. "I've never seen such a beautiful child," she said. "You're very lucky."

"Yes," Vanessa murmured, not knowing what else to say.

"Anyway, I know Mrs. Fitzgerald's anxious to see you both, so let me take you to her room."

A moment or two later Vanessa and Helena were sitting by the bed where Drucilla lay looking pale and weak. "I'm so sorry, Vanessa, to put you to all this trouble," Dru said in a low voice. "What a nuisance I am."

"Don't be so silly," Vanessa exclaimed. "You're not any trouble to me at all. And Helena and I are going to come and see you every day."

Helena said, "And Vanessa says we'll bring you things. Like books and magazines." She smiled at her grandmother. "And flowers, Gran."

"Thank you, darling," Dru murmured.

"Please don't worry about Helena," Vanessa went on, taking hold of Drucilla's hand, squeezing it. "She's no trouble, we'll be fine together."

"But your work . . ." Dru began, looking worried.

"I can do my work and take care of Helena," Vanessa reassured her. "Just think about yourself and getting better."

"I don't know how to thank you."

"Thanks are not necessary, Dru, you know that. And I'm here for you, whenever you need me."

"Bill told me you were a loving woman, and he was right," Dru said. She averted her face for a moment, blinking back tears. Then, turning to look at them both again, she forced a smile. "A hospital's no place for you two. Go and have lunch, and I'll see you tomorrow."

"'Half a pound of tuppeny rice, half a pound of treacle. Mix it up and make it nice. Pop goes the weasel!'"

Vanessa sang, leading the child around the room in a circle, holding both her hands.

Helena laughed, much to Vanessa's relief. She had been in floods of tears all morning, suddenly reacting to her grandmother's departure for the hospital the day before. Drucilla's heart attack, coming so quickly after Bill's death, had been too much for the little girl to handle.

Vanessa understood Helena's concern for her grandmother, but she had not been able to stem her tears, or comfort her. At least not until now. The little game they were playing seemed to have helped. It had brought a sparkle to the child's eyes.

"What a funny song," Helena said. "What's a weasel?"

"A little furry animal with a bushy tail that lives in the woods."

"How do you know this song?"

"When *I* was six, I was living in London for a while with my parents. I had a nanny who was English. She taught me the song."

"Can you teach me?"

"Of course. Sing along with me, Helena. Here we go. 'Half a pound of tuppeny rice, half a pound of treacle. Mix it up and make it nice. Pop goes the weasel.'"

Helena sang with her, and they went round and

round in circles, holding hands. After half a dozen times Helena knew the words, had committed them to memory.

She laughed merrily and clapped her hands. "I'll sing it for Gran when we go to the hospital this afternoon."

"What a good idea, Pumpkin."

The smile slid off Helena's face and she recoiled, gaping at Vanessa.

"What is it? What's wrong?"

"Don't call me Pumpkin. Only Daddy calls me that. It's his name," she cried fiercely, and burst into tears.

Vanessa went to her, put her arms around her, held her close. "I'm sorry, Helena, I didn't know. Don't cry, honey. Please."

But Helena could not stop sobbing, and she clutched Vanessa as if never to let her go.

Vanessa smoothed her hand down the child's back, endeavoring to comfort her, to soothe her, making hushing noises.

After a while the sobs lessened, and Helena grew calmer. Vanessa led her across the studio to the sofa, lifted her up onto it, and sat down next to her. Taking a tissue from the box on the coffee table, she wiped Helena's eyes, then drew her into the circle of her arms. "In a little while we'll go into town and have a hamburger for lunch. How does that sound?"

"Can I have french fries?"

"Of course."

"And an ice cream?"

Vanessa smiled at her. "Yes, if you want."

Helena nodded; then she bit her lip, suddenly looking tearful again.

"What's wrong, honey?"

"Is Gran . . ." Her bottom lip trembled and tears shimmered on her long lashes. "Is Gran going to die?"

"No, of course not! Don't be silly!"

"People die of heart attacks, Vanessa. Jennifer's grandmother did."

"Who's Jennifer?"

"My friend."

"Well, *your* gran isn't going to die, I promise you that."

"But she's in the hospital."

"I know, and she's getting better. I explained to you yesterday, the reason Gran is in the hospital until Friday is because she needs a rest. That's all. Her heart attack wasn't a bad one, honey. Trust me, she'll be all right."

"They're mending her heart at the hospital."

"Yes," Vanessa murmured, giving the child a reassuring smile.

"Gran's heart is broken. It broke the other day. When the men came."

"Men?" Vanessa repeated, momentarily puzzled.

"Daddy's men. From the network."

"Oh, yes, of course."

"They told her my daddy is dead and it broke her heart."

"Yes, darling . . . "

Helena gave Vanessa a piercing look. "Is Daddy in Heaven?"

Vanessa swallowed. "Yes," was all she could manage.

The child continued to look at her closely. "With my mommy?"

"That's right. They're together now," Vanessa said, striving hard for control.

"When is he coming back, Vanessa?"

"Well . . . well . . . you see . . . he won't be able to come back, Helena. He's going to stay with your mother . . . he's going to look after her." Vanessa averted her face, brushed away the tears.

Helena seemed confused. She frowned hard. "I want him to look after me."

"I know, I know, but he can't, honey, not right now. Gran's going to look after you."

"But what if she dies too?"

"She won't."

"How do you know?"

"I just do, Helena."

"Why did the men kill my daddy?"

"Because they're bad men, darling."

Helena stared at Vanessa and started to weep again. "I want my daddy to come back. Make him come back, Vanessa."

"Hush, hush, honey, don't cry like this," Vanessa murmured, endeavoring to soothe her. "I'm here. I'll look after you."

Helena pulled away, looked up into Vanessa's face. "Can we live with you?"

For a moment Vanessa was taken aback, and then she replied, "We'll have to talk to Gran about that."

Helena nodded.

"By the way, where has Alice gone on vacation?" Vanessa continued, wanting to change the subject, distract Helena.

"To Minnesota. To see her mom and her brothers and sisters. Alice has a great-grandmother and she comes from Sweden."

"Tell me some more about Alice."

"Well, she takes me to school and picks me up from school, and she takes me to Central Park and she plays with me."

Vanessa leaned back against the sofa, relieved that the six-year-old was now chattering normally, that she had managed to divert her.

17

On Friday morning Drucilla Fitzgerald was released from Southampton Hospital.

Vanessa and Helena were there to pick her up and take her back to Bedelia Cottage on the dunes. After the three of them had lunch together, Vanessa sent Helena to draw and paint in the studio. She needed to be alone with Dru for a short while in order to talk to her.

"Helena's a lovely little girl, she's a real credit to you," Vanessa said as she and Drucilla relaxed over a cup of herb tea in the sitting room. "We've become very good friends."

Dru smiled and nodded. "I know. She told me, and she sang 'Pop Goes the weasel' for me. She enjoyed herself with you, Vanessa, and I'm so glad she wasn't a problem."

"No, not at all, Dru," Vanessa began, and paused, then said, "But I think . . ." She shook her head. "I was going to say I think there's a problem, but I don't mean that at all."

Dru was frowning, looking perplexed. "What are you getting at, Vanessa dear?"

"I remember that when I was little I worried about a lot of things. All children worry; Helena worries."

"About my health, is that what you mean?"

"Yes. Children can easily feel insecure, and threatened, when a parent is sick or in the hospital. And I believe Helena feels very vulnerable."

"Yes, I'm sure she does, but she'll be all right, now that I'm out of the hospital. However, it'll take her a long time to . . . get over her father's death." Drucilla choked up. It was a moment before she finished softly, "It'll take us all a long time."

"Yes, it will . . ." Vanessa's voice trailed off as she stood, walked to the window, and gazed out at the sea. It was a deep blue on this mild afternoon in early May, streaked with sunlight and no longer bleak and uninviting. In her mind's eye she saw Bill's face; he was never out of her thoughts. She focused on his little daughter, and she knew exactly what she must say to Drucilla.

Turning swiftly, Vanessa came back to the sofa and sat down next to Bill's mother. She gave her a thoughtful look, and said, "Before your heart attack, you told me you had no relatives, and I was wondering if you had ever appointed a legal guardian for Helena?"

Drucilla did not seem at all startled by this question, and she answered evenly, "No, I never have. We never have. It didn't seem necessary. But I know what you're getting at, Vanessa. You're wondering what would become of Helena if I were to die. Isn't that so?"

"Yes, it is. You're a young woman, Dru, and this heart attack has been a . . . well, a sort of warning, I think. I know you'll look after yourself from now on, and you're not likely to die until she's grown. But—"

"You're only voicing what I was thinking as I lay in that hospital bed this week," Dru cut in. "I've worried a lot about Helena, worried about her future. I'm sixty-two, as you know, and I aim to live for a long time. Still, you never know what might happen. Life is full of surprises and shocks . . . "

"Would you consider me? Could I become Helena's legal guardian, Dru?"

"Oh, Vanessa, that's lovely of you to volunteer, but would you want that kind of responsibility? I mean, what if I did die while she's still little? Would you want to care for a child . . . you're young, only twenty-seven, and one day you're bound to meet someone else. To be the guardian of another man's child could be a burden . . . a stumbling block to a relationship."

"I don't see it that way, Dru, I really don't. If I were Helena's legal guardian I would fulfill my obligations to her, no matter what the circumstances of my life. I realize you don't know me very well, but I am sincere and very trustworthy."

"Oh, darling, I know that. Bill loved you so very much, and certainly I trust *his* judgment. Besides, I'm a good judge of character myself, and the day I met you, at Christmas at Tavern On The Green, I knew the sort of person you are. I felt then that a weight had been lifted from my shoulders because I could see how changed Bill was because of you. He was so happy. And I suddenly feel as if a weight has been lifted from me again." Dru took hold of Vanessa's hand and held it tightly; suddenly her eyes welled. She said, "I can think of no one I would like more to be Helena's legal guardian. I know that with you she would always be safe."

Vanessa's eyes were also moist. "Thank you, Dru. As soon as you're up to going to New York, I'd like to make an appointment with my lawyer. Or yours, whichever you prefer. We will set all this in motion. Is that all right with you?"

Dru nodded. "I hope to live to a ripe old age, but it's good to know you're there in the background."

"I'd like us to be together, Dru; I'd like to get to know Helena better, and you too. I was wondering, would you consider spending the summers here with me?"

If Drucilla was startled she did not show it. Without hesitation, she said, "I'd like that, Vanessa, I really would. And I know Helena will be happy. She loves it here."

"Then it's settled." Vanessa leaned closer, kissing Dru on the cheek. "There's something else I have to tell you."

"Yes, what is that?"

"Frank called very early this morning. He's come to New York . . . with Bill's things . . . from his hotel room in Beirut. He wants to come and see us tomorrow. Is that all right?"

Drucilla found it hard to speak. She simply nodded her head and held Vanessa's hand all that much tighter.

"He was my best friend, I loved him," Frank said quietly, looking at Bill's mother. "Everybody loved Bill. He was such a special man."

"He's dead and our lives will never be the same," Dru murmured, her face ringed with sorrow. "But we must go on, and bravely so. That's what he would want."

"Only that," Frank agreed. "He was the bravest man I ever knew. He saved my life. Did you know that, Dru?"

"No, I didn't," she replied. "He never told me that, Frank."

"He wouldn't, he was very modest in his own way—"

"Uncle Frankie!" Helena cried as she appeared in the doorway with Vanessa and rushed forward into his arms.

Frank held her tightly. She was part of Bill, and she looked so much like him, he thought. His throat tightened and for a moment he couldn't speak, so choked up was he.

Frank looked over Helena's head, his eyes meeting Vanessa's, and he nodded slightly. Then, releasing his godchild, he went to greet Vanessa, embracing her. "I'm so sorry, so very sorry," he said.

"So am I," she whispered. "I loved him, Frank."

"I know. He loved you . . . I have something for you." Drawing away from her, Frank reached inside his jacket, took out an envelope. "I found this in Bill's room at the Commodore in Beirut." He handed her the envelope.

She stared down at it. *Vanessa* Bill had written across the front. She bit her inner lip, pushing back the tears when she saw his handwriting. She stared at it for a long moment, afraid to open it.

Dru, watching her carefully, said softly, "Perhaps you'd like to be alone when you read it, Vanessa. We'll leave you."

"No," Vanessa said. "It's all right . . . I'll go . . . outside." She left them in the sitting room and went across the back lawn and down to the dunes, clutching the letter tightly in her hand.

There was a sheltered spot where she often read,

and she sat down there for a while, staring out at the sea, thinking of Bill, her heart aching.

Finally she opened the envelope and took out the letter.

Beirut
Monday, March 25th, 1996

My very dearest Vanessa:

I know I'll be seeing you in a few days, holding you in my arms, but I have such a need to talk to you, to reach out to you tonight, I decided to write to you. Of course you'll be reading this letter when I'm there with you in Venice, since I'll be bringing it with me.

The next few lines blurred as her eyes filled with tears, but after a few moments she managed to recover, and went on reading.

I don't think I've ever really told you how much I love you, Vanessa—with all my heart and soul and mind. You're rarely out of my thoughts and all I want is to make you happy. You've brought me back to life, given new meaning to my life. And now I want to share that life with you. You will, won't you, darling? You will be my wife and as soon as that's possible?

179

In my heart I can hear you say yes, yes, yes in that excited way you have. And I promise you I'll love and cherish you always. You know what, let's make a baby in Venice. I know how much you want a child. And I want it to be mine. I want to know that part of me is growing inside you. So let's do it this weekend, let's make a baby.

I've never told you this before, but in the last six years my life has been hellish. Three people I loved very much died on me. First Sylvie, then my father, and finally my grandmother. Their deaths broke my heart.

But over the past few months I've come to understand that the heart broken is the strongest heart.

Bill.

Vanessa sat there for a long time, holding the letter. And then she folded it carefully, put it back in the envelope, and rising, she walked slowly across the dunes and into the cottage.